ALL ABOARD FOR MURDER

ALL ABOARD FOR MURDER

WELCOME TO LILY ROCK HOLIDAY MYSTERY
BOOK 2

BONNIE HARDY

ON THE OTHER HAND BOOKS

"Christmas is most truly Christmas when we celebrate it by
giving the light of love to those who need it most."

Ruth Carter Stapleton

Along with contests, discounts, giveaways, and events, I'll send you *Meadow's Hat,* a free short story download.
Signup on bonniehardywrites.com/newsletter

ONE WEEK BEFORE CHRISTMAS

Two inches of snow lay lightly on the rough-hewn wood planks that creaked under Michael Bellemare's boots. Crunching his way to the second story of The Fort building, he paused on the landing with a sigh. The crisp scent of freshly fallen snow filled his nostrils as he turned to appreciate the view.

Lily Rock rose majestically in the background, the white cap pointing upward. *This is as good as any place to get through the holidays.* Michael wrapped his arms around his chest, heaving another deep sigh.

Since it was the week before Christmas, fairy lights twinkled on both sides of the town. Mostly from shop windows, outlining the variety of candy canes and snowmen and snowwomen filling the windows. A twenty-four-hour lights-on policy had been adopted by the town council three years ago. That was an exception granted because people flocked up the hill from Los Angeles, taking a day trip to shop and visit Santa. The week before Christmas was the most celebrated and lucrative week of the year, especially for shop owners.

Michael lay his arms on the banister, leaning forward to

look at his latest project. He'd planned and supervised the building of the constabulary across the street, finishing the first phase of construction just in time for the new police officer, Janis Jets, to move in.

He shook his head at the sound of a moan from a loudspeaker, then a series of scratches and scrapes. Without turning around he knew what to expect. *Oh oh, here it comes.* A loud click was followed by the sound of chugging, imitating a train making its way down a track. Then a voice shouted out, "All aboard!"

Michael felt his nerves twinge and his gut clench. He shook his head to clear the ringing in his ears. *Don't bite the hook,* he repeated to himself. That's what he said every time he felt unsettled, especially as of late. A Buddhist pal of his taught him the phrase. He remembered the words exactly: "There's no sense in getting all worked up over the small stuff. Which means the big stuff doesn't matter either. Just don't bite that hook."

"Don't bite the hook," he repeated under his breath. Michael turned from looking at the constabulary to face the storefront. Old Toy Trains, the most opulent shop in town, looked so out of place. Where other businesses seemed low-key and frontier, this one looked as if it belonged in Beverly Hills.

The large window with a stack of boxes holding expensive toy train sets stood alongside a tree with personalized ornaments. One side of each ornament held the store's logo, the other a personalized name. He knew that Betty King, the store's owner, asked a good price to write a name on the back of the ornament. People collected them every year.

In front of the display window, Betty King had placed a wrought-iron bench. She encouraged people to sit there, close to the entrance door. To make it comfortable in cold weather she'd added an outdoor heater, shaped like an old-fashioned street lamp. She'd wound a red ribbon on the pole as a Christmas decoration. Supporting the pole was a large metal canister with a door; tucked inside was the propane tank.

Michael moved closer. Standing to the side of the bench, he looked more closely at the Christmas decorations hanging from the display tree in the window. Familiar names met his eyes. There were several Lily Rock residents with their names on the bright bulbs.

Some people probably order one of those months ahead of time. He looked down, seeing glass jars filled with old-fashioned Christmas candy. Lined up against the window, they made him shudder. Michael's teeth ached at his memory of the sugary crunch and how he used to bite into pieces over and over as a kid.

Removing his gaze from the window, he turned toward the entrance of the shop. A nutcracker loomed over him. The most over-the-top notorious Christmas decoration in all of Lily Rock. The twelve-foot-tall gigantic statue stood at attention. Dressed as a train conductor, the nutcracker stared straight ahead. Michael scowled. That silly oversized shop advertisement for Old Toy Trains had become a bone of contention in Lily Rock right from the beginning.

It looked intriguing and festive, that wasn't the problem. Complete with blue striped hat, bib overalls, brown boots with lug soles, and an old-fashioned lantern clasped in one fake hand, the nutcracker attracted children and adults, captivated by its presence.

It wasn't the visual that had caused the controversy. A loud scratching sound came from the nutcracker, making Michael stare at its mouth. The jaw began to move, exposing a line of very white and even teeth. Then a recorded voice, loud and sonorous, belted out the call: "All aboard!"

That's twice in about ten minutes. The town council told Betty it could only make the announcement once per hour. *Somebody needs to adjust the timer.* He'd been at the meeting when residents first complained.

The Old Rockers, Lily Rock's oldest inhabitants, were the first to make an official complaint. They marched to Betty's shop the week before Christmas and demanded that she stop the racket.

"This is noise pollution," Skye Jones said, pointing a finger at Betty.

"Nobody wants to hear your recording," Doc told her in no uncertain terms.

Betty bit her bottom lip and nodded. "We'll see about that," she told them smartly, before closing her door and turning the sign in the window to Closed. Later that week more complaints came in at the town's monthly meeting.

"That thing gives me the creeps," one woman claimed.

"It's as if her shop is the only one in town," complained the man who ran the candy store.

The intrusive loudness, the frequency, and the sheer audacity of Betty King's advertisement, that was what annoyed the residents of Lily Rock, so the town council made their decision. "Only once an hour, the week before Christmas, then shut it down."

Even tourists were a bit shocked the first time they heard the ear-splitting announcement that spewed from the nutcracker's lips. But no amount of complaining got Betty to back down. "I need to advertise my shop the week before Christmas," she would explain. "I get most of my sales at that time, and I think it's a festive way to bring people to my shop."

Over the last five years Lily Rock residents had grown accustomed to the hourly interruption the week before Christmas. But that didn't mean they liked it. There was something odd about hearing a fake conductor announcing a train that didn't really exist. For Michael it was the sense of being late. The announcement made his heart race as if he had to catch a train, even though he knew it was all pretend. He'd mentioned that to Arlo, the co-owner of the new brewpub one day, when they were looking over the project plans.

Arlo shook his head. "She just makes the recording louder every year." The two men sat at Michael's architectural drawing table.

"I'm surprised the Old Rockers didn't order her to stop," Michael said.

Arlo shrugged. "Let's talk about the outdoor seating," he'd said, changing the subject.

At the time Michael wondered if Arlo knew more than he was saying. But instead of asking, they got back to the plans, making last-minute decisions before they broke ground.

Today the ringing in Michael's ears felt particularly annoying. He slapped his gloved hands together for warmth, waiting for the sound to go away. Walking away from the storefront, he leaned over the railing once again, resisting the urge to keep complaining.

In front of him, a snow plow rumbled past. It stopped in the middle of the road as the man behind the wheel waved at Michael.

"Hey, Brad." Michael waved in return. *That kid has more jobs in this town than a dog has fleas. Probably a good thing. Plowing snow will keep him in weed money for the winter.* With one last wave Michael walked toward the Lady of the Rock gift shop. Meadow McCloud had sent him an early morning text:

Do you have time for a visit this morning?
Lady of the Rock by nine?

Michael rarely refused Meadow, especially when it was only a week before Christmas. Lots of things came up last minute this time of year, no matter how detailed the planning. He'd made himself available on short notice. It kept him busy and stopped him from getting depressed.

And it wasn't just Meadow he wanted to see. Maguire, a year-old labradoodle and Meadow's constant companion, made an early visit sound agreeable. He fingered the dog treats in his pocket as he reached out to open the door to Lady of the Rock.

Maguire had curled up in his bed, near the cash register of the shop. Michael felt his mood shift, calling out, "Hey, buddy."

Maguire stood and his tail wagged. "Bork," he said in greeting. Then he dove under the counter. Only his rear end and tail could be seen. Then he backed out, showing a tennis ball in his mouth. He trotted to the door, dropping it on Michael's soggy boots.

Michael bent over to pick up the ball as a voice from the back of the shop called out, "Good morning, dear." *She's so cheerful all the time.* He tossed the ball for the dog, standing to his full height. Maguire bounced the ball on his boots.

Michael sat down on a stool and then tossed the ball across the room, watching as the dog scrambled past the crystals and books to get to his prize. As Maguire bounded back, ball in his mouth, he dropped it at Michael's feet again. Meadow appeared from around the corner.

"That's enough, Maguire," she said in a stern voice. "No one has the energy to play with you nonstop. Now go to your place."

The dog looked at Michael. When he didn't pick up the ball, Maguire's head hung down. His tail drooped. He slowly walked toward his bed, then flopped down, resting his chin on his paws.

"Our boy seems restless," Michael told Meadow.

"Well that's fine. Most young boys and puppies get bored. He's just going to have to deal with it. He caused me no end of worry a couple of days ago."

Meadow had part-time jobs at Lady of the Rock and the Paws and Pines Animal Shelter. But her main job was being in charge of the town's small library. Michael wasn't certain if she needed the cash or if she just wanted to keep at the center of all the happenings in Lily Rock. Either way he ran into her every day in one place or another.

"Maguire goes with you to all of your jobs?" Michael asked her.

"He likes the animal shelter the best." Meadow nodded. "But he has to learn to get along everywhere else. I can't leave him at home. He's torn up at least a dozen cushions in his crate."

"Not when you're at home," Michael wondered.

"Just when I leave for a few minutes. He's incorrigible." Meadow cast a fond eye toward the dog.

"He's just a puppy," Michael offered as an excuse.

Meadow nodded. "That's why I wanted to talk to you. Do you think you could take care of Maguire at least one day this week? It's such a busy time of year and he'd appreciate hanging out with you rather than me. We're getting on each other's nerves."

"Sure. Glad to help. I'll keep him overnight too, just to give you a break. We can go for lots of walks in the woods."

At the sound of the word "walk," Maguire's head jerked up. His tail thumped against the counter.

"Not yet, buddy," Michael told him.

"I accept your offer," Meadow said instantly. "Let me get his food and toys. I have them in the back. His lead is right over there." She disappeared into the storage room.

Michael stood as Maguire ran to where the leash rested near the front door. Sitting down in front of it, he barked and then turned back to look at Michael as if waiting for a response.

Michael laughed. "Okay, just give me a minute. I want to..."

The sound of the conductor's voice filled the air again. "All aboard!" came his call, followed by a fizzle and then a loud, high-pitched squeal. And then only silence. Michael checked his phone. *Only 9:30. Three announcements in half an hour.*

Meadow came out from the back room with a bag of dog kibble. Flopping it at Michael's feet, she looked at him with startled eyes. "Another announcement so soon?"

"Yeah, it's getting ridiculous." He shook his head. "Maybe I'll take Maguire and mosey on over to Old Toy Trains and ask Betty what she's up to. I'll come by for the food later." Maguire jumped to a sitting position, as if ready for a little excitement.

Michael walked toward the door, the dog close behind. Reaching for the leash, he clipped it on Maguire's collar. He waved at Meadow and opened the door. Stepping outside, the cold stung his face. Maguire raced ahead, pulling on the lead.

"Okay, buddy, I'm coming," he told him, closing the door.

Maguire put his nose down and shook his head. When he raised his head, snow stuck to his snout. Lifting one ear, he seemed to be listening. The hair rose on Michael's neck. *Something feels odd. Even Maguire thinks so.*

"Let's go," he told the dog. Walking quickly, both arrived at the entrance to Old Toy Trains. Michael pulled Maguire in short, his heart pumping.

The twelve-foot nutcracker no longer stood at attention. Face planted in the snow, he looked ridiculous, arms at his side, still at attention. A panel from his back had sprung. Wires spilled out over his wooden legs onto the snow. Maguire growled, pulling at the lead. Michael inched closer, worried at what he saw.

The body of Betty King lay in the snow, one foot sticking out to the side, the rest of her buried underneath the ludicrous nutcracker. It was as if they were kissing, only there was blood next to Betty's head.

Michael reached into his back pocket for his phone, dialing 911. "I need an ambulance at The Fort. Second story, the Old Toy Trains Christmas shop. There's a body. I think it's Betty King. She's unconscious right underneath the nutcracker." Then he hung up. A second call went to Janis Jets, the police officer in Lily Rock. "Get here quick," he told her. "I think we have a problem." He explained what he'd found.

"Death by nutcracker?" came her incredulous voice. "That's gotta be a first. See you in five."

2

THE WEEK BEFORE THE WEEK
BEFORE CHRISTMAS

Michael sat at the round table in the back room of the constabulary. He pulled out a spiral notebook from his pocket to check his list. *If I keep busy, I won't be able to feel sad*, he reminded himself. This philosophy had worked for the past couple of years, as he tried to grapple with his depression.

So far he felt okay. This year Janis Jets was a help. She'd arrived a month ago and his days already felt more full. They'd remained friends over the past year with texts and email.

Finally she got the Lily Rock assignment in writing. She'd shown up within the week, the first official full-time police officer the town had ever known. Half of the community was delighted to finally have a police presence. The other half thought she was entirely unnecessary.

At the sound of Janis Jets coming through the door, he grinned and nodded toward an empty chair at the table.

"Hey, Mike." She smiled at him. "Checking your list twice for Santa?" Jets nodded at his notebook and then walked toward the counter. She poured herself a mug of coffee and turned to him. "Want more?" She waved her mug in the air.

"I just got a refill," he assured her.

Jets sat down next to him, leaning over to look at his list. "So what's that about?"

He closed the notebook. "Every year around this time... Actually the week before the week before Christmas."

"Wait a minute. Is that a thing?" Her eyebrows lifted.

"It is for me. Since Lily Rock amps up their community spirit every year the week before Christmas..."

"With the parade, and the lights, and the candy canes, and all the rest. I think they're having a reindeer exhibit in the center of town this year." Jets shook her head.

"Oh that's not the half of it. There will be bake sales and carolers from the music academy. Everywhere you turn some kid is playing *Jolly Old St. Nick* on their instrument asking for change."

He took a sip of coffee. "So that's why two years ago I instituted the week before the week before Christmas. That's when I check my to-do list preparing to go back to work the first of the year."

"What kind of to-dos?"

She actually looks interested. He felt his gut clench. For a fleeting moment he considered telling her the truth, that Christmas brought up so many memories and even the good ones hurt. *Naw, I don't have to upset her Christmas just because it's a problem for me.* He'd learned to avoid his friends over the years, just to give them the space to enjoy the holiday without feeling sorry for him.

He cleared the lump in his throat. "I have four projects in various stages of development. The constabulary is one of them. I know we're done with phase one, but it's time to make a punch list and get going with phase two."

Jets looked around the break room. "This works for me. I

don't have any staff at the moment. I mean, Lily Rock isn't a mecca for murder and mayhem."

"You've been here a month and are already restless?" Michael's eyebrow raised.

"Once I moved here I thought I'd find a few bad guys. At least I hoped. But after the fire at Lola's nothing has come up. Even the bikers have found another place to drink. Kinda dull."

Her downcast expression made him smile. "So you're the cop who wants more crime?"

She chuckled. "I want to be busy and do the job they pay me for."

Michael grabbed his pencil. "Short of robbing the bank to keep you busy, I do have a plan. So give me your punch list for the constabulary. I'll get it down and then tackle the first task right after New Years. How's that?"

"We can begin with the door," Jets said promptly.

"Which one exactly?"

"The one that separates the office from the cells in back."

Michael scribbled in his notebook as Janis continued to explain. "I need some kind of security. Maybe one of those doors with a keypad or a clicker? That way, when I get an administrative assistant, they can keep surveillance over the door."

"You don't want anyone to walk through unannounced. I get that." Michael made another note on his list.

"Lily Rock is used to going straight to the person in charge. It's a small-town thing that I'd like to change," Jets admitted.

As if on cue, a loud voice interrupted. "Yoo-hoo," she called.

Michael glanced to the doorway. Dressed in knee-high boots, an expensive purple puffy jacket, and skin-tight jeans,

Skye Jones swept her hand in front of her. "So this is your break room. Rather rustic, isn't it?" She addressed Michael. "I thought all of your designs were distinctively modern and sleek."

The hair on Michael's neck rose. He knew he had a problem with Skye. From the first time they met, he'd not trusted her. *She's like a spider that makes me instinctively recoil.* Then to keep himself calm, he added the mantra, *Don't bite the hook.* He forced a smile on his face.

"We were just talking about that." His voice sounded calmer than he felt.

Jets glared at Skye. "So what can I do ya for?" she asked. Her voice sounded caustic and annoyed.

"I want to talk to you about that woman. The Old Toy Train proprietor. She's gone one step too far this time." Skye stepped closer to the table and pulled out the chair next to Janis. Michael felt his gut clench.

"What is it this time?" Jets said calmly. "Has her nutcracker become a nuisance, other than his hourly announcement? I can't do anything about that. I've tried. No one is willing to sign a complaint. Plus the town council gave her the okay."

Skye's eyes flared. "I would sign a complaint without a problem. Except Doc asked me not to. He thinks a softer approach is better. But I'm not so sure."

Michael finished his coffee. He pushed back his chair and stood. "I'll leave you two. I gotta get going to finish by today."

"See you later," Skye said, her eyes on Janis.

Michael walked toward the door. He could hear the two women in animated discussion. *Sounds like they're trying not to argue.* Making his way down the hall, he passed through into the constabulary reception room. Turning around, he stared back at the doorway. *I can measure it now and order the door. It may arrive by the first of the year. That would be a good first step.*

3

AVERY AND LOGAN

The energy downtown felt palpable. More honking from vehicles, more cries from children, more groans from over-wrought parents. Even during the day, lights sparkled from the sequoias at the center of town. Michael crossed the street, dodging an old red truck, the bed filled with statues brought out to install in the park. *I hope they found the baby Jesus this time.*

He stopped at the foot of the oldest sequoia, admiring the thick trunk and stately appearance, especially when compared to last year. After the fire at Lola's, the Lily Rock tree conservation board had taken over the care of the small grove.

They hired an arborist. She instructed the council on how to bring the trees back from near death. Then with plans for the future to make a park, the Old Rockers constructed one oversized wooden table with two benches for people to sit and admire the progress. On top of the table, a plaque had been installed to commemorate Lola's and Old Man Maguire. Those benches would have to do until the spring when construction for pathways and more benches would begin again.

Michael stood holding his hand against the back of his neck as he looked up to admire the highest sequoia branches. Dusted with snow, reaching toward the blue sky, they exuded a sense of calm. He inhaled the crisp air. *I just run out of words to describe this place, how it feels like a cathedral to me.* Aware of a surge of optimism, he rubbed the toe of his boot in the snow. *I can do this. Just keep moving.*

Then he shrugged. *It's no wonder people don't believe me when I try to explain.*

Take Lily Rock, for example. I can't describe her to people who don't live here. I end up sounding like a complete fool. Lily Rock is too small to be called a mountain but too big to be an ordinary rock. What do I say? That there's an entire town named after an oversized boulder with presence?

One time he made the mistake of trying to explain to his friend in Chicago, why he stayed in Lily Rock. But his friend just scoffed at him. "Stop with the nature talks, Bellemare. I get it. Once you've dated every woman in the town and the airy-fairy vibe wears off, you'll be back. Right here at the Chicago office designing post-modern buildings with lots of metal and glass."

Michael's gaze drifted across the open space. As he came closer to the bench, he heard a familiar voice. *Sage McCloud.* As the acting principal of the Lily Rock Music Academy, Sage often counseled the young people in her care. Sitting across the table, two teens looked bored. The boy's leg bounced impatiently under the table. The girl twirled a clump of hair into a corkscrew with one finger.

Sage looked up and caught Michael's eye. A quick dip of her chin indicated she wouldn't mind being interrupted.

Michael walked closer. "Hey," he said. He watched both teens as their eyes lifted to check him out.

"Hey," the girl said dryly.

The boy's eyes met his. He didn't speak.

"This is Mr. Bellemare," Sage began the introduction. She nodded to the girl. "And this is my student Avery Denning, and my other student Logan Tippett."

Most of the boarding students had already left for holiday break. "Heading back home pretty soon?" he casually asked.

"Not me," Logan muttered.

"Me neither," Avery chimed in.

"Their parents have demanding jobs, both in Hollywood. They're on location, so they get to stay with me over the holidays."

"Whatever," muttered Avery.

"Their choice," added Logan.

If not for the disparity of appearance, Michael might have taken them for siblings or at the very least boyfriend and girlfriend. They spoke in an oddly synchronized way, an underlying sense of agreement, especially when it came to their feelings.

"Why don't you sit down," Sage suggested. "In fact you may be able to help me out. Are there any projects one of these capable young people could help you with for the next two weeks? It would be good to keep them busy." She didn't say "and out of trouble," but the implication didn't escape him.

Michael gave Sage a dart-eye. *Under the bus, right in front of the teens. I don't want any helpers. It's hard enough for me to keep my emotions in check this time of year. I don't need two volatile, sad, and hostile teens on top of everything else.* And then because he nearly forgot: *Don't bite the hook.*

His expression must have clued Sage in because she

quickly retracted her offer. "I have other ideas for these two... probably more suitable," she added. "I'm going to send them up to Betty King. She was looking for people to help her with the shop, especially next week."

Michael instantly felt better. "I can walk them up to Betty's right now," he offered. "I wanted to stop in to talk to Meadow anyway. She's spending all of her time at Lady of the Rock since it's close to Christmas."

"Meadow McCloud is also the town librarian," Sage explained to the teens.

Logan spoke up. "What kind of shop does this Betty King run?"

Sage smiled. "You will love the shop. It's called Old Toy Trains. You can imagine the business is especially heavy this time of year."

At that moment a loud electronic crackle came from the direction of The Fort, followed by a loud voice saying, "All aboard!" Then the piercing sound of a train whistle.

Avery put her fingers in her ears. "That's really loud," she hollered.

Sage did her best to keep a straight face. Michael shoved his tongue in his cheek. Logan's mouth hung open. "I like trains. I'd like to find out where that place is."

"I like trains," Avery mocked him. "You would. You're such a nerd."

Michael stood. "Why don't I take these two up to Betty King's?" He turned to the teens. "She's responsible for that loudspeaker conductor recording. It will run every hour the week before Christmas."

"Even at night?" Avery asked.

"It stops at ten o'clock. The town council insisted."

"Why is she playing it now? It's not even the week before Christmas," Logan questioned.

"Betty's getting ready for next week. She's probably giving the conductor tape a test run," Michael explained. Then he turned back to Sage.

"I'll tell Betty about these two potential employees and that they come with your recommendation. Then you can go back to the academy."

Sage's face flooded with relief. "Would you do that? Thank you so much, I can't tell you how helpful that is. I have a mountain of paperwork to look over before I take off for the winter break. And Mom wants me to help her bake the Christmas cookies for the open house boardwalk event next week. And I have to exercise the horses at Paws and Pines..."

Michael felt himself tear up. Despite the rush of words about her to-do list, Sage's gratitude took him completely by surprise. *Look at me and my teeny tiny feelings. Crybaby.* He inhaled, casting his eyes to the side to get control. *Sage is completely overwhelmed. Why didn't I help her out earlier?* He turned to Logan and Avery.

"Come on, you two. We'll head up to The Fort. I'll introduce you to Betty. You may even get to see my favorite Lily Rock citizen."

Logan stood first. "Yah, who's that?"

"A labradoodle named Maguire. He's been getting into trouble lately. I'll explain on the way."

Avery stood. Without a backward glance or a thank you for Sage, she shoved her hands in her jacket pockets. "Whatever," she mumbled.

4
____

BETTY KING

The Fort, decked out in fresh garlands and red bows, looked ready for holiday shoppers. A huge glittering tree stood outside Lady of the Rock. The shop catered to pagan spirituality, but the shop owner made sure that everyone felt welcome, no matter what their religious preference.

Michael ushered Avery into the warmth of the shop first. He stayed by the door as Logan arrived, puffing with the effort to keep up. "Avery has long legs," he explained, looking down at his own scuffed boots. His pant legs folded in accordion-like ripples past his boots to the ground.

"She moves fast," Michael admitted. As he closed the door he caught a look in Logan's eye. Then he glanced at Avery, who stood in front of the incense display. Michael detected Logan's longing immediately, remembering his first crush way back when. *She was tall, taller than me. I remember trying to keep up with her, wondering how I'd kiss her if she were standing. Trying to make opportunities for her to sit down so that I could make my move. Poor kid.*

Michael watched as Logan came alongside Avery. The boy stood six inches shorter, his head barely reaching the tall girl's shoulder. He pretended interest, picking up a package of coned incense and holding it to his nose. Then he glanced to the side to see if Avery noticed.

Michael chuckled. *I took up bowling in junior high, thinking I'd get close to Miranda McBride. It worked, until I saw her older sister.*

Memories of his younger days filled Michael with warmth. He hadn't thought about his teenage years for a long time. He shook off the feeling and called out, "Maguire?"

When the dog didn't come, he looked behind the counter. Maguire's bed lay empty and his tennis ball was missing. "You won't find him, dear," came Meadow's voice. "He went out this morning and I haven't seen him since."

"Went out?" Michael smiled at her. "Someone took him for a walk?"

"He's learned to open the back door in the storage room. He wanders around town looking for people to play fetch and give him treats. Usually someone brings him back. Yesterday Arlo found him hanging out with the workers at the new pub construction site. The day before that Skye entertained him at the doctor's office. She fed him lunch and brought him back."

"So long as people return him, I guess it's okay." Michael felt his gut clench. The memory caught him off guard. He knew the hazards of being there one day and gone the next. *Maybe she's not experienced the loss of a loved one. Every time something good happens, you know what could be waiting around the corner.*

When Meadow stared at him, he forced a smile. *Don't bite the hook, Michael.* He cleared his throat. "I brought two academy students in to meet Maguire."

Meadow turned to look over the shop. "They must be the ones Sage told me about this morning. She's trying to find work for them the week before the week before Christmas."

He nodded, pointing to Logan and Avery, who wandered closer to the table with the rock pendants. Avery held one up to her neck. "What do you think?" she asked Logan. The boy flushed deep red, emphasizing his chubby face and pointed chin.

Michael turned back to Meadow. "Isn't Betty looking for a couple of elves to help out in her shop?"

"She was just in here this morning complaining that she'd been left with only one dependable employee. Why don't you take Logan and Avery over and see if she will hire them?"

Michael 's gaze wandered toward the well-organized display of knickknacks behind the counter. "This place looks great. Very tidy," he commented. "We Three Kings" played softly over a loudspeaker. "You're going all in with the Christmas carols," he added.

"The three kings were magi," Meadow explained. "It goes with our brand."

"Oh right," Michael chuckled. Then he called out, "Avery and Logan. Come meet Meadow McCloud." Avery took the necklace in her palm. Michael watched her with curiosity as she quietly slipped the merchandise into her jacket pocket and Logan's mouth dropped open in surprise.

Gonna nip that in the bud. He cleared his throat and then continued to speak in a loud voice. "It's a good thing the CCTV is up and running this time of year." Meadow, who appeared confused, didn't comment. He added, "No shoplifting in Lily Rock at Christmas. Now that we have a full-time constable, everyone will get prosecuted who gets caught."

It was Logan who reached into Avery's pocket. He pulled out the necklace, placing it back on the table. "Come on," he urged the girl, who scowled back at him.

They made their way to the counter as Michael glared.

Meadow, seemingly unaware of Avery's potential theft, looked serene. "You must be the students from the music academy. My daughter Sage told me all about you. I have a bed made up for each of you at our house. I can't wait to settle you both in."

"Yes, ma'am," muttered Logan.

"Whatever," Avery mumbled. Then she asked, "Where's the dog?"

Logan jumped in. "Avery and I love dogs of all kinds. She has a pit bull at home and I have an English Bulldog."

"My mother took the pit to Switzerland on location," Avery added.

"My dog, his name is Butch, he's at home with the maid," Logan said.

At that moment the front door opened, revealing none other than Betty King. Maguire scooted around her to bound across the room. "Yip," he greeted Michael. Then he sat down to look at Avery and Logan.

"He's adorbz!" Avery bent down to scratch Maguire's head. "Chocolate-brown labradoodles are my favorite. I've heard they are very smart." She bent her knees to bury her face in the dog's fur.

Logan stepped back. His lips turned downward. *Maybe he's feeling a bit jealous at the attention Avery is giving Maguire.*

"I brought back your dog," Betty King announced. "He's a real pest, bothering all of my customers. Today he stood next to the nutcracker, watching people as they came inside. I'm certain he scared away some people. Not everyone loves dogs like you do." Betty glared at Meadow.

"Who doesn't like dogs?" Avery demanded.

"Canines provide human beings with comfort and a sense of security. Studies have shown..." Logan sounded confident, but Michael could hear a tremor in his voice. *Nice job, kid. Defend what Avery loves. You'll never win if your adversary is a labradoodle.*

As Betty shrugged and turned toward the door, Michael intervened. *Maybe now would be a good time to introduce Betty to her future employees.* "Betty, we were actually coming to see you before we stopped here. Do you have a minute? I'd like to introduce you to two potential candidates for part-time work, at least until after the holidays."

Betty King turned to look more closely at Logan and Avery. Logan stood tall, holding his arms at his sides as if being inspected. Avery sat down on the carpet in front of the counter. She folded her legs pretzel style, glaring at Betty as if to say, *I dare you to hire me.*

As soon as she sat down Maguire came closer to sniff her boots. Then he sniffed her cheek and then stepped into her lap to curl himself into a ball. "Good doggie," Avery told him, scratching behind his ears.

"You are both hired," Betty King announced, one hand extended to the doorknob. "Elf One and Elf Two. I have costumes for you to wear. Pay's minimum wage. If you break something it comes out of your pay. And one more thing." She pointed to Avery. "Elf One, you watch for people trying to rip me off and report them." Then she glared at Logan. "And you stand outside next to the nutcracker and welcome people in the door with candy. See you both tomorrow at 9:55. Shop opens at ten and I don't pay for you being early. Not early, not late, but on time. That's my motto."

She flung the door open, stepping onto the boardwalk, and slammed the door behind her. Michael turned to the teens. "Okay then, you can tell Sage that we've got this sorted." When the two said nothing, Michael added, "Can't wait to see you dressed up as elves."

5

MAGUIRE

The next morning Michael lay on his back staring up toward the skylight. Snow had accumulated in the corners of the frosted glass. Blue sky barely peeked through the pine trees, which gently shifted in the early morning breeze.

He'd designed this cabin for himself, as soon as he agreed to oversee Marla Osbourne's more elaborate project nearby. That was before he'd agreed to move to Lily Rock and before he knew that he'd stay, once her home reached completion.

He and Marla originally planned an open house for the week before Christmas. The only problem was that Marla was not feeling very well. She'd been brought down by a respiratory virus that activated her allergies. At least that's what Doc Callahan said.

"We can have the open house anytime," Michael had told her, handing over a mug of tea laced with honey and a table-spoon of bourbon.

"Thanks for this." She nodded. "I don't suppose canceling my open house will be any great disappointment to the residents of Lily Rock." She shrugged, putting her mug down on the table.

"You'd be surprised," Michael said. "They may not accept you yet, but curiosity would bring lots of visitors."

"I'd hire a caterer, you know, give the town some business," she said. "But you're right. I don't have the energy to take on that event. Maybe when I'm feeling better."

Thinking of Marla he realized he hadn't spoken to her in a few days. *I'd better call her and see how she's feeling.* Still in bed, he folded his hands behind his head. Through the skylight he observed a bird balanced on a branch. Hopping from the perch to the glass, it pecked against the ice, making Michael smile. *I suppose I'd better get up.*

He reached over to grab the cell phone next to the bed. One message had come in from Meadow around 5:30 that morning.

> Have you seen Maguire?

He sat up to text back.

> Will check outside in a minute and get back to you.

It's been over an hour. I hope she's found him by now. He swung his long legs over the side of the bed and stood. It had been cold last night, so he wore a hoodie and thick sweats. Slipping his feet into wool slippers, he made his way down the stairs.

Designed as a one-bedroom, one-bath cabin, Michael slept in the loft. He liked the compact plan of his cabin. Having moved from a spacious high-rise in Chicago, he'd come to appreciate having everything neat and tidy and within easy reach.

Glancing out the window facing the deck, he laughed at the two squirrels standing near the feeder. Tails twitched.

One chattered as if to say, *bring on the nuts.* Michael came closer to slide the door open. He stepped outside into the cold as the squirrels ran up a tree trunk. Bending over, he scooped peanuts into an old mug and emptied it onto the wooden tray.

Closing the container, he stepped back inside and heard the squirrels scrambling back down the tree trunk. By the time he closed the door and stood inside, they were both munching on a peanut.

A mug of tea would taste good right now. But I'd better check outside for Maguire. He walked past the kitchen to the front of his house. Opening the door he found Maguire, who had curled up on the welcome mat, as if he could read and took the sign to include him.

"Hey, Maguire," Michael said. "Meadow is worried about you."

The dog sprang to all four paws, his tongue protruding from his mouth.

"Come on in. I have some food for you." Michael held the door open as Maguire walked past him heading toward the kitchen.

Pulling his phone out of his pocket, he texted Meadow.

Your dog is here. I've got him inside.

Immediately his phone pinged.

Relief!

By the time Michael walked to the kitchen, Maguire had already made himself at home. He sat as if at attention, next to the pantry where Michael kept his food. "Okay, I'll feed you, but not until I've made some tea."

It only took a minute to fill the electric kettle with water and turn it on. He plucked a teabag from one of the boxes in his cabinets and dropped it into his mug. Then he bent over to retrieve the dog's bowl from the drawer next to the sink. Stepping closer to the pantry, he found the container with Maguire's food that he'd bought a few months ago. A tin bucket with a top. Scooping the kibble into the bowl, he turned, nearly tripping over the dog.

"I've got this," he said sternly. Maguire sat back on his haunches as if he believed every word. Michael put the bowl down on the floor. "Okay," he told Maguire, watching him spring up to get to his breakfast.

Listening to the crunching, Michael poured boiling water from the kettle over his teabag, filling his mug. He looked out the window over the sink, which faced Marla's house. When she'd suggested that he build himself a cabin, he'd walked the lot and found the perfect location at the back of her expansive lot, giving them both plenty of privacy. The recently installed herb garden, located between the houses, added a buffer. You either had to walk around or walk through two gates to get from the big house to his cabin.

Michael set his mug down. Picking up the phone, he called Meadow.

"Yes, dear," she answered.

"How did he get out this time?" Michael looked at the empty food bowl. "I think he's taking a nap in my bed now," he added.

"Maguire is hard to keep track of nowadays," Meadow admitted. "As you heard, Betty King says he's a nuisance. I wouldn't be surprised if she called animal rescue to pick him up the next time he comes to her shop."

"No way," Michael said. But he had to admit to himself that he could see Betty doing just that. The animal rescue people were notorious for setting hefty fines for dogs they found in Lily Rock. They didn't appreciate having to drive all the way up the hill. "Has he ever been picked up by animal control?" Michael asked.

"Three times," muttered Meadow. "You can bet it cost me a pretty penny. I think Betty would love reporting Maguire, just to make me pay." Meadow's voice shifted. "Maybe Betty's already reported him."

Michael didn't bother to disagree. Betty had a certain way about her that made the hair stand up on his neck. He didn't want to admit she got under his skin, but he didn't want to ignore her either. Not everyone was a kind as Meadow McCloud. Even her harebrained ideas about herbal supplements weren't malicious. She at least meant well.

"I'll keep Maguire for the morning," he said. "Bring him back to you this afternoon. Will you be at Lady or the library?"

"I'll be at the library around two o'clock. And thank you, dear." Meadow clicked off without another word.

6

THORNTON FLETCHER

Later that morning as Michael poured himself a second mug of tea, he heard a knock on the front door. He peered out the window. A familiar truck had parked out front. The knock came again, this time more insistent.

"Bork," came Maguire's announcement. Michael made his way to the front door as Maguire peered down from the loft, his nose poking through a stair rail.

Michael opened the door for the second time that morning.

A burly man dressed in a thick plaid shirt and a black puffy vest stood outside. "Hey, Mike. Got a minute?" Thornton didn't wait for an answer, but walked past as if on a mission.

Michael shut the door. "You want some coffee? I can make a quick pot."

"If you put a shot of something extra in it." Thornton's cheeks were flushed with cold. His eyes nervously darted back and forth as if he had something on his mind.

"Sure," Michael said. "Come on in and have a seat. I'll get the coffee."

"Sorry to come by without calling," Thornton mumbled.

"What's up?" he asked, turning to open the cupboard. Along with an extra mug, Michael took a bottle of whiskey off the shelf. He poured coffee first, then took the top off the bottle. Tipping the whiskey over the full mug of coffee, he stopped. *Not too much. Way too early. Do I need to talk to Thornton about this?* Screwing the top back on the bottle, he returned it to the shelf.

"I've been offered a Christmas job and I wanted to know if you'd let me have some time off from construction, at least until after New Years." Thornton took the mug from Michael's hand, taking a long sip before placing it down on the table.

Michael pulled out a chair and sat at the table. "I think that works. We won't be breaking ground on the pub job until the first of the year anyway. Might even be postponed to spring when the ground thaws."

Thornton nodded. "You gotta take what you can get this time of year."

Michael watched as he took another gulp of coffee. Thornton caught Michael staring at him.

"I've been worried. Our money isn't going as far as it used to. I have some extra bills."

"Is this morning drinking new?" Michael asked.

"Nah. I usually start the day with a shot. It helps with my aches and pains. Cheaper than a prescription. I don't like going to the doc."

"You don't like doctors in general or Doc Callahan in particular?"

His friend looked away, as if embarrassed. "Let's just say neither of us, my wife included, especially like any doc. Keep it at that."

So you're not gonna say any more. And here I thought everyone in Lily Rock loved Doc Callahan. Just goes to show...

When Michael didn't ask another question, Thornton spoke up quickly.

"Thanks, man. I was hoping you'd be okay with it. Betty's paying me triple what I usually make. I can't afford not to take that offer."

Michael's eyebrows raised. "Is that Betty King?"

"She's hired me to play Santa at her shop. And get this. She's hiring Robyn to play Mrs. Santa. All we have to do is walk around during the day and get people to buy stuff. At noon and then four I sit in a big Santa chair. Kids line up to make requests. Mrs. Santa writes them on a paper and then drops them into a gigantic wooden mailbox."

Out of the blue—that was how it always happened—Michael felt emotional. His eyes welled up. He ducked his head away from Thorny. Remembering just a few years ago when he'd last stood in line waiting for Santa. Michael coughed to clear his throat.

"I suppose Betty carries lots of toys in her shop for parents to buy."

"That's my job. I'm supposed to point out all the expensive toys before I sit down as Santa. That gives the parents a chance to buy them when the kids are occupied telling Santa what they want.

"Betty King is a pretty smart cookie. She even keeps her supply of trains and electric scooters out of sight. The parents get edgy, thinking there's only one more, so they need to buy it quick before she runs out. Quite the saleswoman, our Betty."

Michael watched Thornton closely. *I can't tell if he truly admires Betty or if he's scared of her ruthlessness.*

Before he could ask, Thornton took the last gulp of coffee and put the mug down on the table with a thump. "Gotta get going. Betty wants us to work in the storage room until next week. I could make some serious cash if she keeps me until Christmas Day."

Michael felt the back of his neck get warm. It was his body's way of telling him that something was wrong. He thought for a moment before standing up. *Thornton seems a bit desperate, especially drinking in the morning. Maybe I'll check in on him and those two teens for the next several days. Just in case... But I don't have children. What excuse can I use to just drop into a toy store?*

Then he had the perfect idea. "Would you keep an eye out for Maguire while you're working at The Fort?"

Thornton's eyes narrowed. "I suppose so. Is he getting into some kind of trouble?"

"He's running all over town, making Meadow frantic. Plus as soon as Betty catches sight of him, she calls the animal protection people. It's costing Meadow a lot of money to bail the dog out each time. If you could catch him before that happens, Meadow could avoid the fine."

Thornton pushed his chair back, heaving his body to his feet. "No problem, man. Happy to help. Plus I respect that pup! He's actually been coming by our house the occasional afternoon. Appreciates the wife's cooking. She started hanging out with him when she's watching the news. Our whole place smells like wet dog fur." The corner of his mouth twitched. "But I don't mind. Love that crazy mutt."

Michael followed Thornton to the front of the house. Holding the door open, he watched as Thornton walked toward his truck, climbed behind the wheel, started the engine, and then drove away. Seeing his breath in the cold air, Michael closed the door quickly.

Once inside his mind went over their conversation. He shook his head remembering his tears at the mention of Santa and the children. *You gotta keep busy or you'll be blubbering like a fool the closer we get to Christmas. The most wonderful time of the year. Just not for me.*

Rubbing his hand over his eyes, he looked out the window. Snow drifted from the tree branches, light flakes sticking to the glass. For just a moment he wondered about his plan to keep busy. *Should I tell someone how I'm feeling? How I feel every year since...*

Meadow came to mind. *She's one of the good ones.* But then he pulled himself up short. *And for that very reason Meadow doesn't deserve to carry my load along with everything else. Clean up and do something useful, Bellemare.*

He cleared the mugs from the table. After washing them by hand, he wiped them dry. Then he looked around the kitchen. Passing a towel over the counters, his foot grazed the empty food bowl left by Maguire. He picked it up to rinse in the sink.

I'm going to shower and then take a walk into town. I could use the exercise.

"Bork," came agreement from the loft.

Michael shook his head. *Did that crazy mutt just read my mind...*

7

SKYE'S CONCERN

They rounded the corner, walking the last half mile into the town of Lily Rock at a quickened pace. Looking back at Michael, Maguire bounded into the woods. *He must have seen a squirrel.*

"Maguire!" he called out.

The dog disappeared around a tree trunk, snow tossed in the air behind his back paws. Before Michael could call again, he raced back, tail waving in the air. He circled Michael and then came to an immediate stop, his nose next to Michael's right knee.

"Good boy," he told him, snapping a lead onto his collar. Since the complaints about dogs running free, Michael kept a close eye on Maguire, remembering to have a lead handy whenever Maguire showed up. "Let's go," he told him, continuing along the road.

A car beep from behind made Michael jump. He stopped to look over his shoulder. Skye Jones pulled to the side of the road, rolling down her window. Michael walked around the front bumper with Maguire.

"Hey, Skye. You startled me. How are you doing?" He

looked down through the open window where she sat behind the steering wheel.

"Not so good." Her eyes were bright with tears. "I was wondering if Janis told you about my problem."

It took Michael a minute to recollect. Then he remembered that he'd left Skye and Janis in deep conversation the day before. "I haven't seen Janis," he admitted, "but I'm not sure she'd tell me about your concerns even if I had. She tends to keep police business to her herself unless there's a need to know."

"It wasn't exactly police business," Skye explained. "More like town rumor with a twist. I'm quite upset right now."

"Is there something I can help with?"

"I wanted to warn you. I saw you take those two academy students into Old Toy Trains yesterday. Just be careful. That woman is not who you think she is." Skye's voice got intense, as if she were very close to yelling.

"Betty King is a handful," Michael said, hoping a reasonable response would calm Skye down. He didn't want to dismiss her concerns, but he didn't want to activate more hostility either.

"It's not just me," Skye exclaimed. "That King woman is after Doc too. She's spreading all kinds of gossip about the animal shelter. You know he owns that as a nonprofit. I can't believe Betty King—and she's not even an Old Rocker—thinks she can bad-mouth the doc."

Michael instantly realized why Skye was so upset. *She'll do anything to protect Doc Callahan.* Everyone in town knew that Skye's feelings for the doc ran deep and wide. She'd been his receptionist for decades, holding back her love for him just to stay close. *Unrequited love is not fun.*

"I just wanted you to know," Skye said, her lips drawing a

line. Then she rolled up the window, shoving her car into gear.

Michael assumed that was her goodbye. He clicked his tongue for Maguire, who stood up and followed Michael back to the path as they made their way toward town.

Skye's car whooshed past, causing Michael to yank on Maguire's lead. "Stay away from her, buddy," he told the dog. "Something's not quite right, that's for sure."

Ambling down the road with Maguire at his right knee, Michael stopped to admire the town of Lily Rock from a distance. In all of her holiday apparel, he had to admit she was shaping up really well for the week before Christmas onslaught. Getting ready for the perfect winter, the early snow had stuck, providing an inch of cover over the ground.

He admired the greenery that had been hung across the entrance of each small shop. Though the fairy lights weren't visible until dusk, Michael detected their presence, tucked up and woven inside the greenery. The crisp air along with a few snowflakes added to the picture. He brushed the flakes off of Maguire's fur and kept walking. "Time to find you a Christmas sweater, buddy."

Christmas trees twinkled from inside the shops, placed in each window. Even the diner had a tree, hung with spoons, forks, and knives. A gingham cloth had been folded around the base. People walked along the boardwalk, bundled up for winter in earmuffs and vibrant-colored scarves. Michael pulled at his own wool hat. *All of my clothes are worn. I wonder what happened to that crazy Christmas sweater Daniel gave me. He thought that reindeer was so funny. Daniel.* Michael's heart clenched.

He tugged on Maguire's lead. "Let's check on our friends at Old Toy Trains, see what they are up to." He and Maguire took the shortcut through the center of town heading toward

The Fort. Michael stopped to listen. Someone was playing "It's Beginning to Look a Lot Like Christmas" on a tin flute. *Maybe some competition for All Aboard Betty?*

Up the stairs, Michael stood in front of Lady of the Rock. The lights were on in the window, the tree displaying bundles of incense, various crystals, and shiny rocks as ornaments, each hung by a gold ribbon. Gauzy fabric had been wrapped around the tree as a garland. He nodded approval: *very new age.*

Bending over, he spoke to Maguire. "How about you spend a bit of time with Meadow in the shop. After I'm done at Old Toy Trains, I'll come back and pick you up."

The dog nuzzled his hand. Michael dug out a treat from his back pocket. "Here you go." He opened the door, spotting Meadow behind the counter. "I brought your dog," he said with a smile. "If you don't mind I'll come back in a bit and take him with me. He's good company."

Meadow came closer and took the lead from Michael's hand. She unclipped it from Maguire's collar, handing it over to him. "You keep the lead. Otherwise I may lose it." Then she bent over to pat Maguire.

"Hello, dear," she said to him. "Nice to have you back for a while."

Maguire needed no further encouragement. He walked around the counter to circle his bed and they lay down with a humph.

"I've been hearing a lot of banging and moving coming from next door. Probably the storage room."

"One of my crew, you know Thorny, is moonlighting at Old Toy Trains. He told me that Betty had a lot of work for him in back. Once we start celebrating the week before Christmas, he'll be Santa and a salesman too. Along with his wife," Michael added.

"And the two teens. Avery and Logan," Meadow said in a soft voice. Her eyes grew dim, as if she were thinking.

"Anything wrong with that?" Michael inquired.

"I'm getting an odd feeling about Old Toy Trains," Meadow admitted. "I may be biased since Betty has taken such a dislike to Maguire's tendency to wander. But now I'm wondering if there isn't something more."

"I've been feeling uneasy," Michael admitted. "We're not alone. Skye just stopped me on my way into town. She's really upset about Betty and some rumors being spread around town about Doc."

"Is that so?" Meadow's mouth tightened at the corners.

"You're friends with Skye. Has she spoken to you?"

Reaching around the desk, Meadow handed him a plaid envelope. The size of an invitation, he wondered, *Is she inviting me to a holiday party?*

"Open it," she encouraged.

Already unsealed, he slipped his finger inside, edging out a card that looked like a children's art project. *Ho, ho, ho* had been stamped across the bottom of the brown recycled paper in red ink. Above the words, a traditional image of Santa Claus, complete with hat, beard, mustache, and grin, smiled at Michael. Instead of looking festive, it appeared rather sinister, mostly because the Santa image was printed in black ink.

Ho, ho, ho to you, weird Santa. "Do I open this?" he asked Meadow.

"That's the idea," she answered promptly.

Flipping open the card caused a quick intake of breath. Letters had been arranged in words across the blank space. They spelled: *Payment due in three days. Unless you want everyone to know.* He held up the card for closer inspection. "This looks like a ransom note. Like something from an old mystery movie."

"Not quite," Meadow muttered. "More like a blackmailer."

"Sent to you?"

"Not me. But someone who dropped the note in my shop. Maybe fell out of their pocket... Someone who must be feeling very afraid right now, because that was two days ago and the money is coming due."

8

THE ARGUMENT

Leaving Maguire with Meadow, Michael wondered, *Was that card just a prank?* Then he shrugged and removed his punch list to consider his next task. *I talked to Janis already. Once the inner door comes in, I can arrange to have it installed. The next person is Arlo. We're breaking ground early next year, so it would be a good thing to touch base with the Lily Rock council one more time. And then Marla has left me a two-page humdinger of a list. Small stuff to do from painting to removing nails. Plus I want to work on her security system and get the camera going.*

He felt purposeful when he knew he had tasks to accomplish. Five years ago after Daniel's death, he'd gone to a grief counselor. One of the first things she suggested was that he keep busy, especially around Christmas, which was also Daniel's birthday. Her words came to him as if she'd just spoken.

"You'll be reminded of your son especially with his birthday at Christmas. You'll think you're okay, but then it will hit you out of the blue. While everyone else is filled with holiday blessings and cheer, you'll find yourself crying over the smallest things.

"It's overwhelming to lose a child, especially one as young as Daniel. But the tears aren't a bad thing. Just think of them as your love being expressed. Tears are love, Michael," she'd reminded him in their last session. "Keep busy, stay in the moment, make yourself useful. Don't sabotage and avoid the grieving, but don't think about Daniel all the time either. It will get better. I promise."

He shoved the small notebook with his to-do list into his back pocket. *I'll check in on the teens and Thorny and his wife. It's good to be available for other people. Another way to stay busy. Plus Thorny seemed nervous and not himself at my house. I had no idea he was a day drinker.*

One more look at the shop told him that Old Toy Trains exuded the spirit of the season. Every light and decoration was in place. The wooden nutcracker, dressed like a train conductor, stood tall and foreboding, a foot away from the entrance door. Just his size made Michael smile.

He went closer, admiring the construction of the nutcracker. The shiny surface, each paint color distinctly vibrant, including the gloved hand holding the old-fashioned lantern, had been expertly painted. He walked around to examine the back of the pretend conductor. A tall and narrow opening was protected by a tall and narrow door. *A person could fit into the back of this thing. That's probably where Betty keeps the recording device and loudspeaker. Plenty of room for adjustments and repairs, should she require them.*

He walked to stand in front of the nutcracker again. It was only five days until the Lily Rock holiday hubbub started for real: the sound of the conductor, aka nutcracker, would be a constant reminder that the toy store was open for business. "All aboard" an hourly jolt.

Still fascinated by the construction, he ran a finger over the nutcracker's coat buttons. Then a sudden thought popped into his mind. *I wonder if this thing is secured to the deck...* He gave the statue a slight push to test its stability. The nutcracker did not budge. *He seems pretty stable. I'd hate to see him fall on some unsuspecting kid on his way to the toy store.* Michael leaned over to inspect the black boots. Screws had been driven through the paint and then painted over. *Ah, good deal. That should keep him upright.*

Satisfied with the construction of the oversized nutcracker, he turned away. *I'd better go inside now.* He took a step toward the door. His hand froze over the knob. Arguing voices came from inside the shop. Michael recognized the voice of Robyn Fletcher, Thorny's wife.

A quick glance revealed Mr. and Mrs. Santa standing in the corner of the shop, huddled behind the throne where Santa would sit to greet the children. Thornton's eyes locked onto something across the room as Robyn poked her finger in his chest. Her words were loud, almost violent sounding. "My online business is not about you. Stay in your lane, Thornton!"

Michael turned his head. He didn't want to be noticed or to interrupt their personal argument. Standing in front of the window, he pretended to admire the shop's Christmas tree.

He didn't want any trouble, at least not in his state of mind. *I can go inside and get in the middle of something. Or I can wait. Or I can walk away and drop in later.* At that moment Logan Tippett flung open the door. Dressed like an elf, complete with shoes with toes that turned up in the front, he glanced at Michael, smiling with relief.

"Oh hey, Mike," he called out.

"Want to join me?" Michael pointed to an empty bench across the boardwalk. Logan sat right down, exposing his beefy legs encased in green tights. "Nice outfit." Michael nodded to his tricorne green hat with feather.

"Don't start," Logan said grimly. "I had no idea how bad this job would get until Betty handed me the costume. 'Put it on now!' she screamed at me. I mean, nobody does that. She's not my mother. Even my mother wouldn't tell me what to wear."

"She is your boss. At least for a couple more weeks," Michael reasoned.

"I guess," he muttered.

"And you get to work alongside the lovely Avery," Michael added.

Logan's head jerked up. "So you noticed..."

"Who wouldn't have a crush on her. She's beautiful, smart, and a little bit naughty, trying to steal that necklace."

"I guess I'm a sucker for the bad girl," Logan admitted. "But I'm not sure it's worth wearing this outfit!" He looked around and then back at Michael. "So why are you outside?"

"I heard arguing, so I decided to delay going into the shop."

"Oh, that's Thorny and his wife. They've been at it all morning. Reminds me of my parents only worse because they're wearing those outfits." He looked down at his hands. "After hearing them, I don't think I'll ever be able to think of Santa in the same way I used to, you know, as a kid."

And then unexpectedly Michael's eyes teared up. He reached over to pat Logan's shoulder. "Don't worry, kid. Once you get away from this temp job, you never have to take another one like it. I worked all kinds of places before I landed as an architect. You'll get your holiday vibe back soon enough."

Logan nodded. "Thanks," he muttered.

Michael blinked, willing the tears to stop. *Why am I so*

sensitive about this kid getting a dose of reality? It's not like he reminds me of Daniel. Is there such a thing as a grown man being a hot mess? If there is, I must be the poster guy.

He turned back to Logan. "Why don't we walk in together. There's no sense in letting the Clauses keep arguing."

"Every time Betty steps out, they go at it. People look in the window, hear them yelling, and then walk away. If she finds out she's losing business, she may fire them." Logan turned to Michael wide-eyed. "I don't want her to get any ideas and make me Santa. I'd rather be an elf. At least I don't have to have kids pull on my beard all day."

He stood, looking across the boardwalk toward the window. Michael stood next to him. They both listened. To Michael's relief, harsh voices could no longer be heard.

"Let's find Avery," Logan suggested. "She's probably hiding in the storeroom."

"Is she dressed as an elf?" Michael asked.

"Come see for yourself." Logan walked across the board-walk to push the door open.

9

ROBYN FLETCHER

Two days later Michael walked into the Lily Rock grocery. He'd made headway on his project punch list and wanted to celebrate by buying a steak and potato for his dinner. He stood beside the Russets, selecting the largest one to place in his cart.

As he passed the deli counter, he had to walk around the long line of people waiting for coffee. *Lily Rock needs an official coffee shop,* he thought, not for the first time. *Most good coffee shops include a bakery.* He grinned, remembering Meadow's Christmas cookies. *She's way too busy. Someone else though...*

He watched the last woman in the line, who stared at her cell phone. She looked familiar. *That's Robyn Fletcher, Thorny's wife.* Dressed in tight jeans, brown booties, and a black puffy coat, Robyn looked nothing like her Mrs. Claus persona.

"Hey, Robyn," he said, standing next to her.

She looked up, held up a finger asking him to wait, and then pushed Send on her phone. Sliding the phone into her shoulder bag, she gave Michael a smile. "Hey yourself."

She kept talking. "I saw you looking in the window the other day. When Thornton and I were having it out, dressed in our costumes. Must have been quite a sight, Mr. and Mrs. Claus screaming at each other."

"I guess things can get pretty tense the week before the week before Christmas," he said.

"Only one more day and the child rumpus begins. Betty's all ready for the kids and the cash. It seems so backwards to make money on parents, especially those who can't afford her high-end prices."

Michael felt surprised. He'd known Robyn for a couple of years. Seen her with Thorny in town and in line for coffee. They'd never talked about money before. *I never took her for the kind of person who thought about the economics of Christmas.*

"You and Thorny don't have children," he said quietly.

"I guess we're like you, not into babies and all," she responded.

A deep sigh escaped his lips. Another place of sadness released. He never knew what to say in these circumstances. *I had a child once. He died. I was married. The marriage didn't survive his death.* Those were the plain facts, but they never seemed to fit into normal conversations about family.

When he didn't respond, Robyn continued, "Thorny has two children from a previous marriage. We don't see them much, especially since the child support stopped when they turned eighteen."

He nodded. "I've heard that can happen."

She looked up at him, her expression. "You don't have children, right? Did I assume too much?"

Michael froze. He'd led himself right into this conversation. *How am I going to get out of this?* Robyn moved up in the line, giving him a chance to regroup.

"Children are on everyone's mind this time of year," he said.

Robyn, maybe forgetting her question, answered immediately, "You are so right. I've been feeling kind of low since we started this job a few days ago. Thanks for giving Thornton the okay, by the way. We can use the extra cash."

"Expensive time of year?" Michael said, feeling relief that he'd derailed her curiosity.

Robyn's gaze drifted past Michael's left shoulder. She blinked and then focused her eyes on the ground. "We have a new debt that's putting us in the hole every month." Her voice sounded flat. "In fact, that's what Thornton and I were yelling about at Old Toy Trains. It's a soul-sucking payment."

Michael felt his jaw tighten. He used his forefinger to rub the sore spot near his ear to loosen the muscle. *A never-ending soul-sucking payment... Is she talking about being black-mailed?* The image of the macabre Santa card Meadow had shown him popped into his mind.

"I'm sorry to hear that," he told Robyn. She nodded and then stepped up to the counter to give her order. Her back to Michael, she pointed at one sad-looking sugar cookie in the glass case. Gathering her items, she turned back to him.

"I guess everyone has their financial worries. Except you, of course. You never seem to be bothered by money."

"I do have previous earnings that get me past the slow work times. I can design buildings and homes in the winter. Then when it thaws I start construction projects. I guess I'm lucky that way."

"I'm certainly grateful that you've hired Thornton as the foreman on the pub job." The sincerity of her words made Michael feel better. He'd helped two people in Lily Rock and it made a difference.

By the time Robyn grabbed her coffee and cookie,

Michael was ready to push his cart into the checkout stand. "I'm shopping for dinner," he told her. Then he looked at the cart. "Now's the time to tell me you and Thornton want to join me. I can pick up more steaks and potatoes. Are you in?"

Robyn looked surprised. "We'd love to another time. Unfortunately Betty has us working until nine o'clock. Then we open the doors tomorrow at seven. The first day of the last week before Christmas."

"It has become a thing," Michael agreed. "But don't worry. I'll ask again after the holidays. Have fun, Mrs. Claus."

She shrugged, patted his arm, and walked away.

Once he'd checked out, Michael set his bag in the passenger seat of his truck. He felt something near his foot. "Bork," came Maguire's greeting. The dog wore a Santa hat and a bell on his collar. *I wonder how he escaped this time?*

"You look ready for Christmas." He reached down to pat his head. "Why don't you hop in and I'll take you with me." He opened the passenger door. Maguire needed no further encouragement. He leapt from the ground to the seat, right on top of the grocery bag, the tail of his Santa hat covering his nose.

"Oh no you don't," Michael laughed. "No steak for you unless Meadow says it's okay." He lifted the sack, closing the door to keep the dog inside the cabin of the truck. *I'll put the groceries in the back, safe from Maguire.*

To his surprise his contractor's toolbox was open. The lock lay next to the box, as if it had been pried off the hasp. He hopped into the back, irritated. *Who breaks into a truck, especially before Christmas...*

Picking up three hammers and some stray nails, a handsaw and his battery-powered drill, he put them back inside the metal box. *The thief must have been in a hurry. Leaving everything else strewn over the truck.*

After collecting all the toolbox items, there was just enough room to shove his grocery bag on top and shut the lid. *Gotta replace that lock. Maybe after Christmas.*

"Bork." Maguire stood at the back window staring at Michael.

"I know," he muttered. "I'll be right there." He jumped off the tailgate onto the pavement, walking to the driver's side to let himself in. Maguire sat in the passenger seat, facing straight ahead. His tongue hung out the side of his mouth. Then in a surprising act of agility, he moved over the gear shift knob, placing his front paws on Michael's seat. He leaned in to give him a quick lick to the lips.

Michael's mood immediately lightened. *It's as if he knows I need cheering up.* He pulled gently on Maguire's collar, coaxing his paws back into the passenger seat. "I'll open the window so you can say hello to your fans." With the push of a button, the window lowered, and Maguire shoved his head outside.

He watched as two children approached the dog, their mother lagging behind. *Everyone loves that dog. It's as if he belongs to all of us here in Lily Rock.*

10

THE CRIME SCENE

Janis Jets nodded toward Michael. She stood on the second floor of The Fort, wrapped in her black quilted jacket, worn regulation boots planted firmly in an inch of snow. "Nothing says Christmas like a whole bunch of crime scene tape." Jets snorted.

Michael felt remarkably calm, considering he'd found the dead Betty only an hour earlier. He looked at the nutcracker and realized, if he could admit it at least to himself, a certain amount of relief. Finally he'd have something to worry about instead of himself and his Christmas issues.

A quick vision of a nutcracker in a coffin, carried in by Elf One and Elf Two, with Mr. and Mrs. Santa popped into his mind. He shook his head, trying to reconnect with the serious-ness of the situation. *I'm losing it for sure.*

"That was one way to shut him up," he told Jets, nodding at the oversized conductor.

"He was a real crowd pleaser," Jets said sarcastically, "at least for the tourists."

Only twenty minutes earlier Michael had watched the paramedics. They'd gone down on their knees gently shifting the wooden statue up and then away from the body. Tipping the nutcracker to the left side, they propped him up against the building.

Betty King, appearing flattened and small, was exposed. One paramedic on each side, they shifted the body onto a stretcher. An outline where she lay gave Michael a queasy stomach.

He kept watching as one paramedic checked Betty's wrist for a pulse. Once the sheet covered her face, Michael sighed. There was no longer any doubt. Betty King had not survived the crushing blow.

Two people lifted the stretcher as two more arrived on the scene. *Must be the forensics team*, Michael thought. Janis Jets had already stretched yellow tape across the front of the shop. Her team walked under the tape, making their way to the inside of Old Toy Trains while Jets shooed tourists away. "Get out of here," she said. "Go shopping on Main Street. This is a crime scene."

Most people turned away, leaving one woman standing with a little girl's hand in hers. "What about Santa?" The little girl, dressed in a red and white snowsuit, began to cry.

Jets just shrugged, turning her back on the pair.

The mom bent over, using her most persuasive voice, speaking into the child's ear. "Santa is busy right now. We'll come back later."

"But I wanna sit on his lap!" the child insisted, stomping her shiny red boot against the deck.

The mother glanced around to see if anyone else was looking. Michael stared at her, a slight smile at the corner of his lips. "Time for a bribe?" he suggested. "It is the most wonderful time of the year."

The mother snatched her child's hand with an apprecia-tive nod. "Come on, sweetie. Let's get some hot chocolate and a cookie. We can finish the list you made for Santa and then come back." The mother shot Michael a grateful look, making her way toward the stairs, passing other people coming up.

"No Santa this morning!" Jets shouted again. She turned to Michael, mumbling under her breath. "I am not a Santa crossing guard. Get me out of here."

"What about me?" Michael asked Jets. "Should I get going?"

"Absolutely not! You discovered the body and are a main witness." She waved at two more parents with children. "Go away!" Then she turned back to Michael. "Maybe Betty's death wasn't an accident. Death by nutcracker." She paused as if to consider the possibility. "Nah, that's not a thing." She glared at him more fiercely.

She tapped her temple with her gloved hand. "Rumor has it you hated that nutcracker and his obnoxious impersonation of a train conductor. Maybe you arranged for the conductor to make his last announcement and topple over. Betty just got in the way."

He shrugged, turning to face the shop. *Janis isn't wrong. I hated that blaring interruption. I could have rigged the statue to fall over, being a contractor and more than handy with tools.* He didn't bother to defend himself, knowing Jets was just trying to get on his nerves.

When he failed to respond, Jets looked toward the shop window. "The Christmas tree is lit," she mumbled. "Feels kind of otherworldly, the woman who owned the only Christmas shop in town, dying ignominiously under a nutcracker six days before Christmas."

Overhead lights from inside the shop illuminated two police officers taking notes and bagging possible evidence. Michael shifted his glance back to the nutcracker. Propped on its side, eyes level with his boots, Michael felt a shiver up his spine. *Kind of creepy up close. I'm surprised the kids weren't scared of him.*

He noted the array of wires caught under the wooden body. Some tangled between the wooden legs. "Are you looking closely at all of those wires?" He pointed to Janis. "Most of the evidence would be outside, don't you think?"

"Trying to tell me how to do my job, Mike?"

"Oh, I'd never do that, Officer Jets." He mocked her by using her official title.

"We'll get to the nutcracker in a minute. The fingerprint guys are on their way." She stared at him, as if waiting for a comment.

Michael spoke firmly. "I admit I didn't like Betty that much. No one did apparently. But what bothered me the most was that announcement every hour for an entire week. It got on my nerves and seemed to get worse every year. Almost made me want to take a trip to the Bahamas for the holidays. I did hate it that much."

"You weren't the only one." Janis nodded. "But I can't see someone actually bumping off Betty just to shut up a nutcracker announcement."

Michael thought about his feelings. "Killing someone for their insensitive and aggressive business strategy doesn't seem in the wheelhouse of an average Lily Rock resident. Maybe someone from out of town did the job. Pushed the damned thing over just to make it look like an accident. One thing is for sure, it wasn't me."

Jets let a smile break through her serious demeanor. "I never thought it was. Just winding you up a bit. But I do need you to tell me exactly what you saw and why you came over to check out the shop."

"Will there be a hot beverage while I tell you everything, spill my guts, get to the confession..."

"It's always about the tea with you. Let's meet at the constabulary in half an hour. Bring your toolbox along. I want to round up the usual suspects and make plans for my interviews. You can be first. And then stick around."

"What for?"

"You have the perfect cover. You can walk from room to room looking all hunky, pounding in nails and measuring stuff, pretending to do work. But all the while you'll be listening to my interviews. Then we can talk it through afterward. I could use you as a sounding board."

"You can use me as your primary witness, a man with keen observational skills and the desire to bring culprits to justice no matter what the cost."

"Yah, that too." Jets flicked her fingers at him as if to shoo him away.

Michael took the hint. "I'll head over to the constabulary and make you a hair-raising pot of strong hot coffee."

"Hair-raising?"

"Strong enough to grow hair on your chest." He grinned.

"No more about my chest," muttered Jets. "But I would appreciate the coffee. See ya."

11

LISTENING IN

Michael poured the first pot of coffee into a carafe and then set about brewing another pot. He could hear Janis Jets on the phone behind him. Since the interview rooms were not fully equipped, she'd created a makeshift worktable in the break room.

"Are you done yet?" she snapped. "I need coffee. Rounding up these suspects is like pulling teeth. I wish one of them would just say, 'Sure, what time?' But oh no. They have to start the interview on the phone, nattering on about the dead woman, when I'm not ready."

"That must be a pain," Michael said. He brought over two mugs of coffee, putting them on the table. Then he returned with the carafe. "I don't even like coffee," he admitted. "I just say I do because people expect it from a construction guy. I stopped by the market and picked up some fake cream and sugar to add to mine. Makes it palatable. Just in case I'm making some for other people. Should anyone stop by." His voice dropped at the end.

Jets looked at him over the brim of her mug. "We'd certainly not have become friends had I known your distaste right in the beginning. A guy who puts cream and sugar in his coffee is a deal breaker."

He returned with the carton of cream and a sugar bowl. "So does this mean the friendship is off? I should have known." He shrugged, pouring more cream than usual into his mug. He looked up. "I hope that made you squirm. Wait, I'll put in lots of sugar too. If you get queasy, feel free to leave." Without even a smirk, he put four heaping teaspoons of sugar into his mug and began to stir.

"You still drink beer, right?" she said, sounding serious.

"Still do." He smiled at her.

"All right then, I will turn a blind eye to your unfortunate coffee habits."

Michael took the first sip from his mug and put it back on the table. "So tell me, how long is your list of suspects?"

Jets opened her iPad. "I've got everyone who worked at Old Toy Trains lined up. I figured I could begin there and see if it led to someone else. I'm also waiting for confirmation from the coroner. I may be able to call this an unfortunate accident and close the books. It depends on what they find."

"So there are ways to tell if the nutcracker just toppled over by accident?"

"They can tell a lot of things by looking at Betty's body."

He took another sip. "It does seem to be the worst sort of luck for Betty to be walking past that nutcracker right when he fell over. I mean, that just feels like some kind of other-worldly redemption."

"Makes me want to live it up more," Jets admitted. "You never know how much time you have."

"Speaking of time," Michael said. "Before I look at your list, how are things going with the new job?"

"Been here a couple of months. This is my first case. Don't know yet."

The short sentences made Michael curious. *Is she happy here?* Janis shoved her iPad across the table for him to read her list.

"So you've got the two elves, Logan and Avery. Then Mr. and Mrs. Santa, Thornton and Robyn." Michael was surprised at the next two names. "And you included Skye and Doc Callahan."

Jets reached over to take her iPad. "Yep, they aren't employees, but they had a beef with Betty King. Skye's been at me for weeks to get involved. And now I don't seem to have any choice."

Jets's phone pinged a message. She looked over at the screen. "Looks like the coroner has a preliminary report. I'll talk to her and get back to you."

Michael pushed back the chair to stand. "I'll go get my toolbox and start with the punch list. Do you want me to work in here first, just so I'm hanging around?"

Jets held the phone to her ear. She nodded to him as she said, "Janis Jets here. What do you have for me?"

* * *

By the time he returned with his toolbox, Jets had cleared the table of coffee mugs. There were the same two chairs but this time spaced farther apart. She looked up. "So Betty died on impact. The damned nutcracker struck her on the head and killed her instantly. What are the chances of that?"

Michael put down the toolbox to seriously consider. *I didn't like Betty that much, but she didn't deserve to go that way. I wonder if there was something seriously inadequate about how the nutcracker had been secured. It seemed solid enough when I took a look, but I may have missed something.* He shook his head, feeling a lingering sense of guilt.

"I had a close look at that monster a couple of days ago," he told Jets. "I thought it was pretty secure. Huge wood screws driven into the planking from the top of the boot. Very professional. Whoever installed the thing had painted over the heads on the screws so that they didn't show. I gave it a test shove and it didn't budge."

"And in answer to your question, why don't you get to work in the other room and then I'll text you to wander in looking all nonchalant. You can pretend to hammer stuff over there." She pointed to shelving that had been stacked on the wall. "Remember that's where I wanted the storage to be?"

Michael nodded. "Oh I remember. You know that's not in my job description. I'm the construction engineer, ready for the big installations. I'm not a finish carpenter."

"Who cares. I'm not an administrative assistant either, but here I am taking my own notes, sitting in a break room without a decent place to interview a potential murder suspect."

That's what's been bothering her. I knew it was something. She's impatient with the constabulary facility. I can get on that. Michael turned away from Janis, looking for a place to put his toolbox. He set it on the floor next to the kitchen counter when he heard someone calling from the hallway.

"Hello, anyone here?" Skye Jones appeared in the doorway. She wore her blonde hair back in a ponytail, along with a bright red form-fitting sweater. Her jeans fit her snugly, emphasized by knee-high black leather boots. Her lipstick matched the sweater, as did the red scrunchy she'd used to wrap around her ponytail.

Michael sniffed. The essence of strawberry, like added apparel, wafted in with Skye. Not a perfume as he surmised when he'd first met her, but her favorite flavor of vape. "Hey, Skye." He pocketed his tape measure when she wasn't looking his way. "I lost my tape measure," he called out, "have to search the truck."

Jets eyed him and nodded. "Happy you're finally finishing up that shelving unit." She glared at him for effect. Then she turned to Skye.

"Come have a sit down," she said. "I want to catch up on your concerns regarding Betty King and find out if there's any connection with her death."

As Michael walked down the hall he wondered, *Does she think Skye may have something to do with this murder? That would be surprising. She's an Old Rocker and would have other ways of getting Betty out of town. Not renewing her business license for one. That's the usual way.*

He pivoted in the hallway and took out his tape measure. Stepping back into the room, he held it up high just in case Skye wanted to know why he was there. When she didn't turn around he raised an eyebrow in Jets's direction. When she blinked in response, he walked quietly to the other side of the room.

Jets cleared her throat. "So tell me more about Betty and Doc."

Good acoustics. I didn't deliberately plan for the break room to be good for eavesdropping, but I can hear them talk just fine. Michael strapped a tool belt around his waist, listening carefully for Skye's response.

12

───────────────

A CASE OF SLANDER

"Oh, Doc doesn't have anything to do with this," Skye insisted.

"That's not what you told me last week. You came right in here and said that Betty King was trying to coerce money out of the doc to keep quiet regarding Paws and Pines."

Michael swallowed hard, turning his back to the two women across the room. *I don't think Skye will realize I can hear every word. But what's that about Paws and Pines...*

To anyone paying attention, Michael might have been mistaken for an overgrown naughty schoolboy sent to the corner for misbehaving. He hovered in the corner, his back to the women across the room. *I feel like a cat trying to hide behind the curtains with his tail sticking out for everyone to see. But so far Janis isn't addressing me, so I'll keep pretending to look in my toolbox.* He inhaled deeply to calm his nerves.

"Please tell me everything you know that the doc is keeping secret about the animal shelter." Jets's voice sounded firm.

When Skye didn't respond right away, Michael bent over his toolbox to find a piece of sandpaper. He stood up and ran the paper against the wall, still on alert.

Skye's voice trembled. "As you know, the doc is a man who devotes much of his time to charity. He works countless hours down the hill at the Native clinic for women and children. And then he's our Lily Rock resident doctor three days per week."

Jets growled. "I'm not doing a job interview here. We all know Doc's a great guy and how he gives money to small businesses and causes. Especially here in town. He's part owner of the new brewpub project and an Old Rocker. Blah blah blah. What I want to hear about is the animal shelter."

Michael kept sanding the wall, minding his own business, waiting for Skye's response.

The topic of Paws and Pines was not new to him. It so happened that he and Janis were together just a year ago when they'd wandered about Paws and Pines together. In the search for the baby Jesus statue, they'd come across boxes of CBD supplements and bottles of red pills filled with diphenhydramine, a well-known over-the-counter antihistamine.

Janis voiced her concern later, after she'd been hired. "Don't people use diphenhydramine to put themselves to sleep?"

"Sometimes people give half a tablet to a kid just to make them stop coughing and of course, to get some sleep themselves," Michael added.

"I don't know about kids," she'd said at the time. "But Paws and Pines is the quietest shelter I've ever been to. Dogs don't bark even when people come around to visit." When Michael just shook his head, Jets added, "Somebody needs to look into that."

Michael lifted the sandpaper off the wall, realizing the repetitive scratching had caused him to check out. Now there was an uneven dip in the wall's surface. *I'll cover that later.*

Won't show after I paint. Better start paying attention to what I'm doing.

"Dr. May runs a very efficient animal shelter," Skye said in a loud voice. "But Betty King thought otherwise. She'd found out about a few complaints."

"What do you mean, complaints?" Jets's voice lowered.

"A few people misunderstood Doc's use of perfectly natural over-the-counter remedies. He's a qualified doctor, you know, even if not for animals exactly. But those complainers couldn't leave well enough alone."

"So Betty found out. Did she put in a complaint herself?"

"No, but she accused Doc of drugging the animals at Paws and Pines. She told him she'd tell everyone in town that he'd been officially warned by the animal rescue people too."

"I haven't been here long, but I know how the people in Lily Rock love their animals. Especially dogs, they just go gaga over Maguire. So maybe Betty had a point. Maybe Doc needed a reprimand, or at least a callout from his community." Jets's rational summary made no difference to Skye.

"How could you say that!"

Perhaps sensing a further reprimand from Doc's favorite fan, Janis changed course, this time in a calm voice. "Okay, so you don't agree with me. No problem. I can talk to the animal rescue folks down the hill if I want more information."

At that moment Michael snapped his tape measure closed. "Ouch," he said aloud. His thumb began to bleed.

"You okay over there?" Jets asked.

"Got some blood. I'll rinse it in the sink." *I can spend some time rinsing and looking for a Band-Aid. Plus it's closer so I can hear better.*

Skye didn't even look up, she kept defending the doc. "I think Betty King slandered the doc and that she wanted to undermine his reputation in our community. That's not legal. That's why I came to you."

Jets cleared her throat. "And like I told you before, defamation of character claims are very hard to prove. On the one hand, I suppose Doc has a lot of money and that he, if anyone, could take Betty to court and most likely win. But on the other hand, I think Betty was right. Doc had been cited for drugging the animals. He'd have a hard time proving he was innocent if what she said was actually true."

Michael watched out of the corner of his eye. Jets tapped her fingers on the table. "So where were you yesterday morning, from nine to ten o'clock?"

"I was sitting behind my desk in the doctor's office," Skye responded promptly. "You can ask Doc. He's my alibi."

Jets must have had enough. She snapped, "And you bet I will ask Doc. And I'm going to look into the Paws and Pines complaints while I'm at it. We're done here. Plus I have another interview coming up." She closed her iPad with a nod.

Skye stood up as her cell phone rang. She answered as she walked toward the door. "Yes, how are you, Marla? Another appointment? Still feeling under the weather. Have you taken those supplements Dr. Callahan prescribed? I know they're expensive. That's why we'll help you grow your own herb garden in the spring. Meadow is on board to talk to you after the holidays. But until then you have to buy the prescribed herbs from Meadow."

Michael kept listening. *She's talking to Marla. I haven't seen her for a few days. Sounds like she's still not feeling well.*

As Skye exited through the doorway, Jets pointed toward her back, gesturing for him to shut the door.

Once he stood by the table, she spoke first. "I don't have another interview today. I just told her that because she was starting to annoy me with her *Doc is so wonderful* talk.

Starting again tomorrow morning at eight o'clock. Can you get here by then?"

"Sure." He held up his sore finger. "This may be a workman's comp situation. Are you prepared to pay?"

She laughed. "Don't bother with the paperwork. I'll bring my Scooby Doo *brandaids* tomorrow."

He laughed, walking across the room to gather his toolbox as Jets made notes on her iPad. He turned around when he heard her ask, "I have a good notion to call the doc in for questioning. Any thoughts?"

Michael paused. "I'm not sure that would go well. He's an icon in Lily Rock and you might stir up more confusion, which won't help with this particular case."

"My thoughts too," Janis confirmed. "But so you know? I'm going to look into the Paws and Pines situation the first thing next year. Something is not right there."

13

A PUBLIC NUISANCE

A text from Janis Jets woke Michael the following morning.

See you at eight. I want you to sit at the table. I'll explain when you get here.

Got it

Stretching his hands behind his head, Michael stared at the skylight and then the pine ceiling. He'd carefully designed the rough-hewn boards in a diagonal pattern, knowing that he'd be looking up from his bed most mornings.

A bump to the foot of the bed brought his glance downward. "Okay, Maguire. I'll get up. Come here, buddy."

The dog leapt to the bed to nestle close to his body, his nose poking into Michael's ribs. Maguire had spent the past three nights with him. Meadow signed off as soon as she heard the dog was in safe hands. "He's not mine," she reminded Michael. "I just took him through the first year. You can have him now if you want."

The sharing attitude had surprised him. He made an extra

trip to town to buy more kibble and an oversized dog bed, which he kept in his bedroom.

Absentmindedly scratching behind Maguire's ear, Michael felt some anxiety. His first thoughts went to any outstanding bills. When he assured himself he'd paid all the November receipts, he thought about his punch list. *I have plenty to keep me busy with the constabulary. The rest may have to wait until after the holidays.* His heart felt light, his breathing regular. *Something's missing though. I wonder...*

He scratched Maguire's neck some more. Then it hit him. His eyes flew open. *I don't feel sad this morning. What happened to that gut-wrenching guilt I was running away from just a week ago?*

He explored his feeling of unfamiliar calm. *Will this last? Nah, the guilt will come back.* He'd only have to think about Daniel. The boy's clear blue eyes and seven-year-old grin. The way he said "Dad." Michael felt a lump in his throat. Then he inhaled slowly and calmly. *Just missing Daniel, but no guilt.*

"Love you, son," he said aloud.

Maguire lifted his head, planting his chin on Michael's abdomen. He scratched the dog's head. *You're good medicine for me, Maguire. You keep me company. It's like you know that I require some managing.*

Heaving himself out of bed, the dog wiggled over to lie in the warm spot. "You stay there while I shower. Then we can go to the constabulary. Officer Jets has an assignment."

On the way to town Maguire sat in the passenger seat, his head hanging out the side window. "It's cold in here," Michael complained. "Can I close the window now?" When Maguire did not pull his head back, Michael pulled his coat closer. "I guess it won't be much longer." *And I'm talking to a dog like he's a person.* He shook his head, feeling chagrinned.

Janis Jets was ready for him when he walked into the

break room. This time three chairs stood around the table. She sat in one taking notes on her iPad. The aroma of coffee filled the room. "Mug ready for you over there. Cream in the refrigerator," she mumbled, eyes still on her work.

Maguire trotted with Michael toward the sink.

"I didn't invite the mutt," Jets said.

"He doesn't care," Michael commented. Walking back to the table, he sat down. Maguire edged his way under the table to lie on his feet.

Michael reached into his pocket for a dog treat, which he slipped to Maguire.

"If he gets caught in town without a lead, I'll arrest him." Jets sounded confident.

"Not if you want to remain friends with Meadow," Michael reminded.

"The dog could be a public nuisance," Jets said.

"Or the greatest asset Lily Rock ever had. A free-range labradoodle who loves tourists and shows up to greet everyone with a smile."

"Sounds more like a politician," Jets mumbled.

And that's an interesting idea all in itself. Maguire the politician. Maybe I can float the suggestion at the next town council meeting. I know Meadow would approve.

Jets cleared her throat, looking up from her iPad. "So I called the doc and did an informal phone interview. He assured me he wasn't planning on taking Betty King to court and that he was used to a little criticism. 'You're nobody unless somebody's suing you,' he said, and that's a quote."

"Who's coming in for an interview this morning? And why am I sitting at the table, not lurking in the corner with sandpaper?"

"I decided to fully engage your listening skills this next time. No more eavesdropping. I'll introduce you as voluntary constabulary staff and just see if anyone disagrees. You're kind of official."

"Do I get a badge or a whistle?" Michael looked hopeful.

"You get to be quiet and not ask questions," Jets said. "When the interview is over, then I'll run stuff past you."

"That's when I point out anything you've missed," he concluded.

"No, that's when you make more coffee. Geez, give a moose a muffin."

Michael felt a pang. *One of Daniel's favorite books,* If You Give a Moose a Muffin. *We laughed at the moose every time. The loss filled his chest, making breathing difficult. And just like that I'm back to grieving.*

"Are you ready for me now?" Avery stood in the doorway. Her tall, thin body, dressed in jeans and a bright blue puffy coat, made her look younger than her sixteen years. She came closer to the table, flashing a brief smile at Michael.

"He's helping with the interviews," Janis explained. "Have a seat."

Looking calm, her dewy skin smooth, her gaze cast downward. He could not imagine Avery would mean anyone any harm. Until Janis Jets asked her first question. "So I heard that you've been stealing from Betty King ever since she hired you last week."

Avery looked up and then directly at Janis. "Stupid Logan. I told him not to tell. I didn't take that much. Just small stuff. It's not like there's anything in a toy store that would interest me. Plus I hate trains. And the kids begging their parents for toys and a chat with Santa? It gets old."

Michael lifted his hands and folded them in front of him. Maguire shifted, easing himself out from beneath the table as if to catch a better look at Avery.

Her eyes lit up. "Hey, doggie. I didn't know you were here." She reached down and scratched his head.

Maguire leaned into her fingers, enjoying the attention. When she stopped scratching, the dog walked to her side and laid his head in her lap. Avery's body listed toward the dog, her hand caressing his side.

Michael reached into his pocket, sliding a dog treat over the table toward her. "Give him that. I can see that he really likes you."

Avery snatched the treat, holding it in her palm. She lowered it closer to Maguire, who took it instantly, returning his chin to her thigh.

Avery began to speak, her voice softer, less defensive. "I did steal stuff, but I didn't have anything to do with Betty's death. She didn't even know my name, called me Elf One. She was just a ridiculously bitter woman who thought running a toy store would disguise her suspicious and mean heart. And her real business, which wasn't toys. Kind of sad really."

Jets tapped her fingers. "What do you mean 'real business'?"

"Oh come on. Lily Rock isn't that blind. I even heard the rumors and I've only lived here since the fall. Betty King has some kind of black market business and she's connected. You know. To the Mafia." Avery's voice quavered. "I didn't want to cross her, that's for sure." Michael watched her hand reach out to pet Maguire.

Jets made a note in her iPad and continued. "Okay then, on the one hand you don't mind ripping off your employer, especially if she's known to be crooked. But on the other hand you suspected that she was up to something and just kept quiet.

"What I'm wondering is how much did you really know about Betty's supposed real business?"

Avery didn't hesitate. "She sent notes to people in town. Blackmailed them about personal stuff, I think."

Michael's head jerked up. He remembered the note with the Santa on the front and the *ho, ho, ho* printed underneath. Dropped in Meadow's store. Along with Skye's testimony, Betty the blackmailer sounded true. *I wonder who else Betty threatened and collected money from?*

14

WHERE'S MAGUIRE?

Jets leaned toward Avery, her eyes bright with anticipation. "So Betty King was blackmailing people... Do say more."

"I was told to keep quiet. But then she's dead now, so I guess it doesn't matter." Avery's speech quickened. "Probably one of those people, the ones she blackmailed, they killed her. Or maybe her mob connection wanted more of the share of her business and was tired of her stingy attitude. Either way she was a horrible woman. Makes sense that someone would eventually bump her off."

"Not someone, but who specifically do you think would kill Betty?" Jets sounded impatient.

Avery, seemingly aware of the attention she'd attracted, leaned back into her chair, looking confident. Her voice came slowly as she explained. "It only took me a day to see Betty for who she was. People coming to the counter. She'd take them in the back room. They'd leave with an envelope clutched in their fist. Happened over and over.

"And then she took Logan aside. He told me later she insisted that the job of Elf Two was to stand inside that stupid nutcracker and listen to people's conversations while they sat on the bench getting warm. He was supposed to report back to her at the end of the day."

"Did he record the conversations?" Jets asked.

"He remembered most of them. Wrote some in a notebook. People would sit on that bench and jabber and he'd just take it all in. He spent most of his time inside that nutcracker," Avery admitted.

Jets cleared her throat. "And what about the notebook?"

"Betty must have taken it from Logan and then used the information to blackmail people. Not everyone gave in, but a lot of people did. They'd come over when Santa and Mrs. Santa opened for business. People would casually hand an envelope to Mrs. Santa. At first I assumed they were paying for the toys. But then I remembered Betty would insist that no money changed hands in the shop. She did everything by card. That's when I got more suspicious and put things together."

"So the Santa couple was in on the blackmailing?" Jets's voice held an edge.

"I liked Mr. and Mrs. Santa, but they sure looked like part of the blackmailing to me. Kinda made me even more sad about Christmas." Avery frowned.

Michael felt a pit in his stomach. *Thorny and Robyn. I don't believe it.*

"So tell me, who handed over those envelopes?" Jets asked.

"I only paid attention at first," Avery said abruptly. "I don't know the people who live in Lily Rock. Most of them are strangers to me." Her face was blank.

Michael looked closely at Jets. *Is she thinking what I'm thinking? Avery may have conspired with Betty. Maybe she was willing to help out with a little blackmail on the side.* Michael's jaw clenched. Janis's eyes narrowed. She stared back at him.

"Thanks for this information. I'll bring it up to Logan when we get together. Then we'll get his point of view."

"Oh, he told me everything," Avery said at once. "He kind of has a crush on me, so he used it as an excuse to chat me up."

Michael sighed. *Logan wouldn't be the first teenage boy to get in trouble because of a girl.*

Jets shut down her iPad. Before she could speak, Maguire stood and let out a "Yip!"

"Somebody out front?" Michael asked.

"The door's unlocked," Jets said. "Why don't you have a look?"

Maguire glanced back at Michael and then trotted to the door. His paws skittered on the flooring. Michael called out, "Maguire," but the dog began to run, bolting down the hallway.

Michael ran after him calling, "Maguire. Buddy!"

"I'll get Elf One here to sign a written statement of her interview. I'll text you when we're done here," Jets yelled.

Making his way down the hall, he stopped at the entry door. No dog in sight. When he reached for the doorknob he realized that the door had been left ajar. Stepping outside, he looked toward the busy street and then back at the library. No sign of Maguire.

Michael glanced across the street. *I'd better check the park first.* He waited for traffic to pass and then ducked behind a bumper to sprint toward the sequoias.

Two children stood in front of a snowman, placing a scarf around its neck. A woman nearby clicked photos, calling out advice. "Smile, Kim. Stop scowling, Matthew." Walking past the photo op, Michael looked toward the wooden bench. A couple sat facing each other. They had their mittens wrapped around steaming cups of hot chocolate.

Michael turned to look back across the street. He shook

his head in disbelief at what he saw. The animal rescue van, pulled along the curb, looked out of place in the festive Christmas atmosphere. *Has someone already told them about Maguire?* He crossed the road, dodging slow-moving traffic as he ran zigzag toward the van.

He peered inside the back window. *No Maguire.* Michael walked around to the driver's side. The open window showed a guy sitting behind the wheel, slumped back into the seat. "Have you seen a labradoodle about a year old?" Michael asked.

"You mean that crazy Maguire?" the guy retorted. "I haven't seen him, but I'd know him. We've picked that dog up half a dozen times. I wish someone would keep track of him. He's becoming a nuisance."

"So no one called you about Maguire?" Michael wanted to make sure that he'd heard correctly.

"Naw, we came up the hill for a Christmas cookie and a coffee. Lily Rock is pretty this time of year. But we'll grab a stray if we see one. Can't be too careful with dogs. And don't forget the coyotes. They get overconfident this time of year. Might try to go after a domestic dog or cat to eat and then scare the kiddies."

Despite the dire warning about the animal food chain, Michael felt relief. "Talk later," he mumbled, taking off toward The Fort. *Maybe Maguire went back to see Meadow.* Climbing two steps at a time, he made his way to the second floor. Then he walked inside Lady of the Rock.

Meadow stood behind the counter. She looked surprised to see him. "How are you, dear?"

"Is Maguire with you?" He shut the door behind him.

Meadow looked alarmed. "He's not here. I thought you had him."

"He bolted out of the constabulary like he'd seen a squirrel or something. The animal rescue van is on the street, but they haven't seen him either."

Meadow came around the counter. "We'd better find him before they do. I'm afraid he's been picked up so many times, they may cite me for negligence."

"You stay here. I'll keep looking." Michael spun around and bolted out of the door. He walked past the Lady of the Rock window display and around the corner, coming face-to-face with the crime scene at Old Toy Trains.

The nutcracker, appearing relatively unscathed, was still propped against the side of the building, where the paramedics had left it. Its position made it look like an oversized decoration waiting to be packed away after Christmas. Michael scanned the statue when his eyes stopped at the large black boots. He stepped over the crime scene tape to examine more closely.

A gaping hole appeared in each black boot. Someone had removed the bolts. Michael noted the rough wood inside the hole. *Whoever unscrewed those bolts must have been in a hurry.*

He looked through the shop window. Without lights the place no longer held its festive allure. No Santa to welcome children, the train on the shelf near the ceiling had stopped moving. Even the caboose hung precariously, two wheels off the track.

Sunlight illuminated the decorated window, shining a light on the Old Toy Train ornaments dangling from the branches. The names were still visible. Doc and Skye. Thornton and Robyn. Other names that Michael didn't recognize.

The hair on his neck stood up. *Wait a minute. Do those ornaments have any significance? Could they be the names of people Betty was blackmailing? Right in plain sight as if to taunt her victims.*

He returned his attention to the nutcracker. *I wonder if someone sabotaged that nutcracker, unscrewing the bolts to make it fall. That would explain why it toppled over. Maybe they hid behind it and waited, and when Betty came out the door, one big shove and down it went. Did they intend to kill Betty or just injure her as a warning to back off?*

Michael's phone pinged inside his pocket. He pulled it out. A text from Janis Jets.

Get over here now. Forensics just sent me their initial findings. This was no accident.

15

SANTA PAWS

Back at the constabulary, Michael half expected to see Maguire. But no sight of the dog. Just Janis Jets sitting at the table in the break room. She looked very serious.

"Have a seat." She kicked the chair next to her. Michael sat down. "Where's the pooch?" she asked.

"Can't find him anywhere," he sighed.

"Okay then, we'll look later. I have something to tell you about the investigation." She shoved her iPad toward him. He began to read.

Once done, he shoved the iPad back. "So Betty King's death wasn't an accident."

"That's right. Blunt force trauma by nutcracker." Jets looked serious but Michael suspected she was doing her best not to smirk. Despite the serious implications, the entire scenario felt unworldly. "Something about the nutcracker being sabotaged," Jets added.

"I saw it for myself. When I was looking for Maguire, I took a look at the murder weapon."

"It's not..." Janis stopped herself. "But I guess it is. Death by oversized nutcracker. Bizarre but accurate. So what did you see?"

"The bolts that were screwed into the boots had been removed. Looked like a hurried job too. Mostly yanked. Lots of torn-away wood. Someone used an electric drill. I have no doubt that once the bolts had been removed the statue became unstable." He stopped to think and then asked, "Did the team happen to find the bolts?"

"We aren't amateurs," Jets reminded him hotly, "of course they did. Got them both bagged and they are at the lab being checked for fingerprints."

"That may reveal the murderer," Michael said. "Unless the person was wearing gloves." He scratched his head. "Anyone check CCTV?"

"Betty didn't pay for closed circuit cameras," Jets said. "I suspect she thought cameras unnecessary because she trained her staff to watch for thieves. What with Elf Two hidden in the nutcracker and her three employees circling the shop, she saved money by doing it the old-fashioned way."

Jets looked at her phone and then back at Michael. "So the interview with Avery was revealing. I'm starting to think Logan is a serious suspect. His job was to stay close to that nutcracker. He could have unscrewed the bolts after the shop closed or early that morning before it opened. Instead of stepping inside, he may have waited behind the nutcracker and then shoved it on top of Betty when she came outside."

Michael nodded. "He admitted to me that he has a thing for Avery. Maybe he observed her with Betty and thought he was saving her from a life of crime. That day I took them over for the job interview, Logan watched Avery steal a necklace at Lady of the Rock. He took it from her and replaced it before she could object."

"A regular knight in shining armor." Jets looked grim. "I hate it when teens get into big trouble."

"Are you going to interview Logan today?"

"We're scheduled for tomorrow morning. I know he's at Meadow's house. I told her to keep an eye on him. She said she'd report any odd behavior. Speaking of the interview, can you be here? You seem to have a soft spot for the kid."

"I was wondering, is it okay for you to interview under-aged kids without an adult or attorney or parent present?"

"Well that's the thing, Mike. You're the adult. Their parents are 'on location.'" Jets used finger quotes to emphasize "on location." Then she smirked. "If Logan turns out to be the murderer, we'll call in an attorney and notify the parents. Then I'll track down their whereabouts. I don't care where Mom and Dad are, I'll find them."

Michael nodded. "So who's left to interview after Logan?"

"Thornton and Robyn. They seem to be in the thick of this mess too," Janis said.

"Yeah, Avery seemed to think so." Michael thought back to his conversation with Thornton in the kitchen. He'd seemed concerned about money. *Betty paid him a lot to be Santa. That's why he wanted the job.*

Jets interrupted his thoughts. "Santa and Mrs. Claus may have been co-conspirators, running a blackmailing scheme in plain sight."

"So I was wondering..." Michael's voice trailed off. Then he cleared his throat. "The tree in the window at Old Toy Trains? It has personalized Christmas decorations with the names of Lily Rock residents. I wonder if that was Betty's way of alerting the people who owed her money? She hid their names in plain sight until they paid."

"That's pretty imaginative." Jets nodded. "It even sounds like Betty. Obvious and kind of clumsy, with the Santa notecards and back room talks. I could see her doing that with the ornaments. I'll have someone on the team go back to the shop and collect them, just to take a closer look."

I'm glad I mentioned that. Maybe I've finally added something important to the investigation. "Okay then, I'll continue my search for Maguire." He stood to leave. "See you tomorrow."

Once outside the constabulary, Michael looked past the library toward The Fort. People crowded the boardwalk, many holding the hands of children, their arms filled with gift bags. He felt the now familiar pull on his heart. *The holidays will never be the same for me. Every child I see reminds me of losing Daniel. And I feel vulnerable for the parents who can't even imagine that their children could die.*

I don't want to go home.

He pulled his coat closer, zipping the front. *Without Maguire, I'll just think about my own problems and get depressed.* With a sigh, he stopped to look through the Lily Rock Library window. No Meadow behind the desk because she spent the week before Christmas at Lady of the Rock. *Maybe I can pick up a few gifts at The Fort just to keep busy. Sage and Meadow and Janis for sure.*

He entered the throng of people walking past the library, taking slow steps to match their pace. Stopping at the window of the Lily Rock Mercantile, he looked inside. A big smile came to his face. The shop proprietor had placed a glass container labeled Dog Bones at the far end of the checkout counter. People stood in a line that stopped just short of the entrance. In an orderly fashion, people peeled off the line, making way for the next customer. The woman in front lifted her child, who reached into the jar. She lowered the boy to stand on his own feet, bone clutched in his small fist. The child leaned closer to the dog as he offered the bone in an outstretched hand.

Maguire wore a red and white Santa hat. Once he'd finished chewing he lifted a paw that the boy took. The mother lifted him up again, turning to walk away as the next person stepped forward. Then Michael saw a sign that read, *Stop and shake the hand of Lily Rock's famous Santa Paws. Make a donation to animal rescue on the way out.*

Michael opened the door. *No dinner for you tonight, buddy.* He entered the shop with a grin. *Now that's what I call ironic.*

16

WHERE'S LOGAN?

Michael brought Maguire into the break room. He'd slipped a lead from his pocket, hooking it on the dog's collar. Walking to the counter, he started to make a fresh pot of coffee. Maguire yanked at the lead. Michael dropped it. "You can go lie down, but I'm leaving this on just in case you try to run away again."

Maguire shook his head and then turned his back on Michael to look toward the corner.

He's annoyed and ignoring me. That's okay. He spoke to Maguire's back. "I want to keep you safe and out of the hands of animal rescue." He chuckled as he turned back to run water for the coffee.

That dog belongs to everyone in town. The lead isn't a permanent solution, but it will have to do until the holidays are over. Then we can figure out how to keep him from being apprehended. How is it that Maguire's worst nemesis, the animal rescue, are the very ones who are making money with his Santa Paws handshakes?

Jets walked into the room looking grim. She clicked off her phone. "So that was Meadow," she explained.

"And..."

"It seems Logan ran off in the middle of the night. She's gone through his room to see if he left any clues as to his whereabouts. She found something of yours under the guest bed."

Michael felt the hair on his neck raise. "And what would that be?"

"An electric drill."

His eyebrows rose. "That surprises me. I keep it in my toolbox and it's locked, right in the back of the truck." Then he stopped, realizing that wasn't necessarily true. "Except for a few days ago, when I found my toolbox had been broken into. The lock had been tampered with. Nothing was missing though. At least I thought my drill was right there in the bottom, under the screwdrivers and hammers."

"Meadow says your name is on the drill."

"I do have my name engraved on my more expensive tools."

Jets came closer, holding out her empty coffee mug. "Logan was my first appointment this morning. He's run off, which makes him look really guilty."

"Does that mean we'll send out a search party for the kid?" Michael pointed to Maguire. "He's ignoring me," he explained. "But I'm sure he'd love a good search party. Maybe then he'd forgive me for keeping the lead on his collar."

Jets laughed. "Let me make a few phone calls. Then we can begin a search. Maybe the mutt will come in handy. Does he know Logan?"

"He does." Michael looked pleased. "They bonded that first day when I took Logan and Avery over to meet Betty King." He walked closer to the dog. Reaching out, he patted Maguire's haunch. "Wanna go outside, buddy?"

At the word *outside*, the dog leapt to all fours. Spinning around, his tail wagged over his head. Michael scratched behind his ears. "I'll finish with the coffee. And then we'll see if Maguire is a good tracker."

Jets nodded. "But first we'll stop by Meadow's house. She's gone to work, but Sage is home on her winter break. She'll show us the kid's room and your drill. Once you identify it as yours, we'll have an important clue for forensics. Maybe they can match the drill to the bolts we found at the crime scene. And hopefully there will be fingerprints."

Michael's stomach dropped. "It sure looks like Logan is our culprit. Maybe he ran away because he didn't want to face you this morning. You are pretty scary."

"I am supposed to be scary," Jets insisted. "It's in my job description. Terrifying suspects. I practice looking formidable in the mirror every morning." Jets swept her hand over her body. "I am a lean, mean constabulary queen."

Turning his back on Janis with a chuckle, he reached up to open a cupboard. By the time he found a travel mug and filled one with fresh coffee, Jets was calling impatiently from the doorway.

"Let's go, Mike. And don't forget the mutt."

Sage opened the door wearing fluffy slippers and a sleepy smile. "I wasn't expecting visitors this morning," she explained, "until Mom called."

Maguire walked in first, trotting ahead toward the kitchen. Michael and Janis lingered to chat with Sage.

"Have you heard from Logan?" Jets asked.

"I haven't seen him since last night." Sage pointed to the hallway. "Avery is still sleeping in the office on the pullout. Do you want me to wake her up?"

"We talked to her already," Janis said. "Let her sleep a little longer. Then I'll question her. Logan may have told her where he was going."

"Logan left all his stuff," Sage said. "You can come see for yourselves. I tried texting him an hour ago but no response."

Jets looked toward the hallway. "Okay, let's check out his room first."

Sage led the way.

At the first step into the guest room, Michael smiled. A fluffy bedspread decorated with snowmen lay in the middle of the unmade bed. Crochet doilies covered the dresser and bed stand. Jets pulled back the covers, releasing the smell of teenage boy, part sweat and part cheap aftershave.

Michael rubbed his nose as Sage cracked open the window over the bed. "Meadow left the drill where she found it." She pointed and Janis lifted the dust ruffle off the bed. With a tug, she pulled out the drill. Standing up, she handed it to Michael. "This the one?"

It only took a second. "It's mine. I was sure it was in the toolbox, but I must have made a mistake."

Jets pulled a large evidence bag from her backpack. "I'll bag it and get it to the lab. You can stay and talk to Sage. I'll be back in fifteen minutes to look over the rest of the room and to interview Avery."

"I can feed Maguire breakfast while we chat," Sage suggested.

"He's been eating his weight in dog bones all over town," Michael said with a frown.

"Then I'll give him half a scoop of kibble," she replied, as they heard the sound of the front door closing.

Sage led the way to the kitchen where they found Maguire standing in front of the pantry. He'd spent the first year with Meadow in the kitchen, being fed and house-trained, where she kept a good eye on his growth. He did not turn around when they came into the room, his gaze glued to the pantry doorknob.

"I guess he's hungry again." Michael grinned.

"I'll get his food. You have a seat." Sage reached for a metal bowl and opened the pantry door. Michael watched as Maguire walked inside. He nosed the large bag of dog food and then looked up at Sage. She unclipped the top. Pulling a half-filled cup out, she dumped it into his food bowl.

Outside the pantry Sage placed the bowl on the ground. "Okay," she told Maguire. He leaned over the bowl and began to munch.

Michael looked out the window. Snow still rested on the branches of the pine trees. The space through the branches exposed blue sky. "I like this view," he told her. Sage looked over at him and then sat down, her eyes inquisitive.

"What's going on with you?" Sage got right to the point.

"Just the usual." He smiled, looking away.

"I've known you for a few years now," Sage explained, "you always seem a bit down this time of year."

"I'm not a big celebration guy when it comes to Christmas." He tried to sound light but suspected Sage wasn't fooled.

"Not everyone loves the holidays," she agreed. "But you're not your usual self. I saw Marla the other day and she said you'd barely spoken to her for the last couple of weeks."

He dug in his pocket, pulling out his pad of paper. "She's next on my punch list. I got caught up at the constabulary and I didn't get to her as soon as I wanted to."

"See, that's what I mean. You are keeping deliberately busy with non-Christmas tasks, as if you're running away from something. We notice, your friends care about you. You know that, right?"

Tears stung his eyes. He swallowed hard, clearing his

throat. "Okay, so you're right. I am trying to get through the holidays and it's taking all my willpower. I didn't realize it was so obvious."

She reached out to touch his arm. "To your friends. Not everyone, but we care about you."

He nodded. "I'm not ready to talk about it. But so you know, there's nothing anyone can do. I just have to wade through and make the best of things. You help, Meadow helps, even Janis brings me moments of cheer." He pointed to Maguire, who stood by the back door. "And that big mutt is no end of comfort. He's sticking pretty close to me lately. And he's amazing company."

Sage stood and reached her arms around him. "How about a hug then? Probably better than a lot of words."

He pulled her close as her head tucked under his chin. Her clean hair held the hint of lavender. *Of course she smells like lavender. She's Meadow's daughter after all.*

Still holding her, his heart rate slowed. He closed his eyes and inhaled. Sage's words ran through his mind, making everything, at least for the moment, a little bit better. *We care about you.*

Despite his attempts to keep busy and distant, he knew the truth: *I care about all of you too.*

17

ACCESSORY TO MURDER

Michael and Maguire arrived at the constabulary at ten o'clock. The streets held several tourists who waited outside for the shops to open. *Only two more shopping days until Christmas. And then I'll be through all of the holiday whoop-de-doo for another year.*

"Excuse me," a woman said, nearly colliding with him on the boardwalk. She smiled, displaying attractive dimples on her smooth young cheeks. Dressed in a snug-fitting quilted coat with a fur hood, she looked directly into his eyes. At another time he might have taken her interest and responded with a bit of mischief of his own, but not this time. *I'm not in the mood for flirting.*

Hoping that she'd get the message, he glanced down at the boardwalk. Once he'd gathered his composure, his eyes traveled back up, where he noted a purse that she possessively tucked under her arm. He blinked. *I think that's a genuine crocodile bag. Look at the gold clasps. Not like I'm an expert, but I remember women buying those in Chicago. Very classy and expensive.*

Stepping around the woman and headed toward the

constabulary, Maguire trailed behind. Once through the entrance he dropped the dog's lead. Maguire took that as a signal to move ahead, his tail waving from behind. He disappeared down the hall as Michael closed the door. This time he made sure it was securely latched.

Michael smelled the coffee, already brewing from the break room. *I guess Janis got here early.* He had appreciated the time at home, looking over his to-do list and preparing for the emotional upheaval the next couple of days would bring.

Christmas Eve would be the worst. But by the time he got to Meadow and Sage's house for breakfast Christmas morning, he'd be tired but ready to take on the rest of the year. The memory of Sage's hug helped. *I do have friends. Maybe one day I'll tell them why I'm such a moody bastard over the holidays.*

Hearing the door behind him open, Michael turned only to feel relief. Thornton, his hand firmly grasping Logan Tippett's elbow, spoke up. "I think this guy is a day late for his interview." The teen hung his head.

"I'm sure Officer Jets will be happy to see Logan," Michael commented dryly. "And when she's done, I want to know how my state-of-the-art electric drill found its way under his bed."

Logan's head dipped further as if he felt contrite. *It may be an act.* Michael felt his jaw tighten. *That's better. Don't let your weakness show. The kid could be a killer.*

Janis Jets appeared in the doorway. She did not look amused. "Give me that kid," she told Thornton. Jets didn't wait for Logan to come closer. She walked over and to Michael's surprise, turned the kid around and clipped a pair of handcuffs around his wrists. "Logan Tippett, you are being taken into custody for not showing up when I asked for an interview, and for inconveniencing a police officer."

Inconveniencing a police officer. Is that a thing? Michael didn't let on that he doubted Jets's tactics. Instead he watched as she marched him through the doorway. "You two follow me." Jets's voice came from around the corner. "I'm going to tuck Logan up in a cell. See how he feels about that!"

"Come on, Thorny," Michael urged. "I smell coffee. You can tell Jets what you know. We'll get to the bottom of this."

Thornton, Michael, and Janis sat at the table, and Janis had already pulled out her iPad. She looked over at Thornton. "So where did you find the kid?"

The big man sighed. "He's been at my house the whole time. Me and the Mrs. kinda took a liking to Elf Two at first. He seemed lonely and lovesick. I wasn't around much with my kids, when they were his age. At least I'd show up for Christmas. What kind of parents are they? So Logan, he reminded me of me when I was his age—awkward, girl crazy, and insecure."

"And Robyn, did she feel the same way?" Jets asked.

"Yah, she did. Robyn has a soft spot for kids. Even though she didn't want any of her own, she can't stand to see anyone take advantage of children, even teens. Especially teens. She didn't like the way Betty pushed him around and made him stand in that damned nutcracker for hours at a time spying on people. She worried that the kid might suffocate in such close quarters.

"I taught him how to drill holes into the nutcracker for air and for him to see. If you look carefully, each one of the big buttons has a hole drilled right in the center. Logan looked out from there, and it lets some air inside so that he could breathe."

"Sounds like workplace harassment," Jets mumbled. "Why didn't the kid complain?"

Thorny leaned forward, folding his hefty arms on the table in from of him. "Well that's the thing. We realized pretty soon that Betty hired us because she knew we wouldn't squeal. We noticed her side hustle the first day. It took some time to realize all of her employees were scared of her, and she'd threatened all of us so that we'd do her bidding."

"On the one hand everyone in Lily Rock has a side hustle to make ends meet," Jets said. "Typical small town. But on the other hand, I get the feeling that Betty was blackmailing people, and that's not just a side hustle, it's illegal." She frowned.

"I know," Thornton mumbled. "But we couldn't say anything."

"What did she have on you?" Jets looked calm, but Michael knew she was onto something important. He'd realized in the other interviews, by watching her carefully, that her eyes gave her away. Her pupils pinpointed Thornton like a cat watching potential prey.

Thornton's mouth closed tightly. It appeared that he was not going to answer Janis's question. She waited but to no avail. So she opened her iPad and made a few notes. Once she finished, she looked up again. "If you're covering for Elf Two in there, you'd better come clean. Keeping quiet and not answering my questions makes you look very suspicious. I can arrest you for being an accessory to murder. Unlike inconveniencing an officer, that is a real thing." Her voice crackled, making the hair on Michael's neck stand up.

Thornton squirmed. "The kid has nothing to do with Betty's death." He turned to face Michael. "A couple of days ago he came to tell me that the bolts in the nutcracker boots had been removed. He asked me what to do, so I gave him my drill and told him to put the bolts back in. It happened a couple more times. As soon as Logan showed up for work he'd find the bolts removed. I had to keep giving him bigger ones so that they'd grip the wood."

"Why did he steal my drill if he had yours?" Michael asked.

"I have no idea," Thorny replied quickly. He looked away, over Michael's head, as if he were nervous.

"Didn't you wonder why the bolts kept being removed?" Michael asked.

Thornton looked back at Michael. "I thought it might be vandalism. I knew how everyone in Lily Rock was sick and tired of that all aboard announcement coming every hour for an entire week. I mean, Betty just ignored everyone's complaints. So I thought someone finally got sick of it and undid the bolts, you know, just to make a point."

Michael inhaled deeply as Jets typed into her iPad. She looked up at Thornton. "I'm going to write all of this down in a witness statement for you to sign. But I am warning you now. It's what you're not telling me that will bring you down. You are holding something back, mainly why Betty King hired you in the first place. She had something on you and I want to know what."

Thornton crossed his arms in front of his chest. He shook his head. "I just can't tell you. Not because I don't want to, but it's not my business. Robyn and I keep our financial lives separate. Things have been tight so I've taken over a lot of the bills. But I never ask her why."

A look of surprise came over Jets's face. She raised her eyebrows at Michael.

Did he just give away what he'd been trying to keep back this whole time... That Robyn had a financial problem but not him?

Jets nodded. "Keep your finances separate, you say?" She tapped the table with her fingers. " I'm going to arrange an interview with Robyn, just to see what she has to say about all of that."

18

—————

KNOCKOFFS

The next day Michael hurried across the street with Maguire close behind. They headed toward the constabulary. It was already ten o'clock and he knew Janis would be waiting impatiently. She'd texted him:

Where are you?

As his foot hit the boardwalk, he heard a scream. Stopping in his tracks, he looked toward The Fort and shook his head in disbelief. A woman with a black coat hovered threateningly over another woman wearing red.

The black-coated woman squeezed her hands around the neck of the other, whose back had been thrust against the railing. Another scream made him shudder as he watched her arms flailing in the air as she tried to catch her balance.

"You're going to pay for this!" the assailant screamed.

Worried that the woman would fall over the rail from the second story, Michael sprinted into action. Heading through the line of traffic, he narrowly missed the front bumper of an SUV. Once in the clear, he broke into a run.

Horns honked as Maguire ran closely behind, fast at Michael's heels.

Once Michael reached the stairway he took two steps at a time, dropping Maguire's leash. At the top of the landing he found one woman on her back being strangled. The woman in a black coat on her knees, her fingers wrapped around the other woman's throat. And then a third woman, wearing a yellow parka, stood to the side calling out, "Keep squeezing," to the woman on top.

Michael ran toward the black-coated screaming woman. Bending over he grasped her hands and wrenched her fingers free from the victim's neck. She tried to shake him off, but he held her arms firmly.

He dragged the assailant to her feet. She yanked her arm again, this time pulling away from his grasp. Michael watched her closely. When she didn't go back after the other woman he said, "Stay back there. I'll see if she's okay."

The black-coated woman complied, her friend's arm around her shoulders.

At first the victim curled up into a ball, lying in a fetal position. But then she rolled up to a sitting position, her purse clutched in her hand. He took a step back to give her some room. Once again he eyed the black-coated woman and her friend to make sure they were keeping clear.

By now people from the town had stopped shopping to watch with interest. It wasn't every day that three women, obviously dressed expensively, physically fought in public.

"Step back and give them space," Michael urged, moving to block the assailant and her friend from the victim. No one came closer, so he turned slightly to check on the victim. "Do you need help? Should I call 911?" Before she could answer, a familiar voice interrupted.

"All right, move aside, move aside," came the firm voice of

Janis Jets. He could see her head and then body appear at the top of the steps. "What's going on here?" She stepped in front of the battered woman, kneeling down to look her in the face.

The woman still held her purse close to her body, her face streaked with tears. "I don't know what's going on. Both of those women came out of nowhere and just started attacking me, hitting me with their purses. Look at my head!" She pointed to a bump that had begun to trickle blood. "And then that woman in the black coat tried to choke me to death."

"Do you know these ladies?" Jets asked.

"I've seen them around," the woman said in a lower voice.

Then the assailant spoke up.

"She knows us, don't let her say otherwise." Up closer, Michael could see that she wore an expensive-looking black suede coat, belted at the waist. A bright pink leather purse hung from her shoulder. "And I want to lodge a formal complaint."

Jets stood up straight. "You don't get to lodge a complaint. She's the victim!" In a loud and certain voice, Jets added, "And you could have killed her!"

Michael blinked. *Am I seeing things?* While Jets had been talking he'd noticed that both the victim and the assailant carried the same style handbag. *Kinda pricey, crocodile leather is expensive.* His eyes took in more detail. The other woman standing next to the assailant also had the same handbag. The long strap handles looked identical in shape, plus the feet on the bottom were brass. All of the bags were the same rectangular shape. The only difference was the color. One bag was pink, the other green, and the last silver-gray.

I'm not a purse specialist or anything, but that seems very odd to me. He spoke up. "Officer Jets. Can we talk?"

Jets's head jerked around. She began to shake her head *no* but then stopped. "Excuse me, ladies. Don't move. I'll be right over here with my eye on all three of you." She came closer to Michael. "What do you want?"

"There's something weird about those three," he whispered in her ear.

"Just spit it out. I don't have time for theatrics," Jets growled.

"Look at their purses."

Jets's face froze. Staring at one woman, then the next, she shrugged. Then she nodded. "Those are Birkin bags," she told him.

"I saw a woman earlier with the same style handbag. Now these three women, that makes four in just an hour. What's a Berlin?"

"That's a *Birkin,* not a Berlin. Very high-end. Eighty-five hundred for the cheap ones. They go up in price to over a hundred grand. Even Walmart handles Birkins online—thirty thousand each. Only the very rich and the wannabe rich can afford them."

"So all of these women have similar expensive brand bags..." Michael knew better than to make fun of a woman's handbag.

"Now that's what I'm wondering," Jets mused. She went back to the group.

"Alright ladies, I can't help but notice all of you are carrying a Birkin bag. Very nice, especially this time of year. Does that have anything to do with the battering and assault of this woman?"

"She told us ours were knockoffs!" The woman in the black suede coat pointed at the victim in red. "She had the nerve to point out how the brass feet at the bottom of my bag weren't hammered in and that only the fakes had screw-in feet."

Jets's mouth tightened. She spoke to the woman still

sitting on the wood deck. "How do you know these women aren't sporting the real deal? Are you some kind of expert?"

Despite her bruised face and the blood now trickling from a wound over her temple, the woman held her own bag in the air triumphantly. "This is a real Birkin. My husband bought it for me in Europe. Look at the distinct green color. Plus I know the difference because I am a handbag collector." She gestured with her brightly manicured forefinger. "Those women have fakes. They're not the only ones. I've been in town for a few days and I've seen any number of Birkin knockoffs on women's arms. Fakes, every single one of them."

Jets nodded and then turned back to the three women. "So where did you get your Birkin bags?"

"Right here in Lily Rock!"

"We got them from the same place. The lady who dressed as Mrs. Claus at that shop." The assailant pointed to Old Toy Trains. "After the first time, we came up together to get gifts for friends."

"So you all paid Mrs. Claus..." Jets mused. Then her hand reached around to ease her backpack off her shoulder. Michael grinned as she looked at the beat-up exterior and the one strap hanging by a thread. *Not exactly Janis's deal, expensive handbags.*

The friend of the assailant let out an exasperated sigh. "We'd walk through the shop and pretend to look around. Then Mrs. Claus would meet us in the back storage room. We'd hand over the money and she'd give us the Birkin. When we said we were satisfied, she tucked the purse inside an Old Toy Trains shopping bag. No one even looked at us as we exited the shop. Mrs. Claus said we were getting the highest end bag for a mere four grand."

Michael's jaw dropped. Robyn was the instigator of this scam?

His thoughts were interrupted when the assailant's cell phone chimed. She pulled it out of her bag and silenced the alarm before shoving it back.

Jets tapped at her iPad. *She's biding her time, maybe wondering if she should arrest these women.* When Janis finally looked up, it seemed to Michael that she had made her decision. "I have another inquiry that requires my immediate attention. I am going to write down everything you said. And then I'll take your names. If you want to press charges about your fake Birkins or the assault, you can find me at the constabulary. It would mean reading over the statements and signing them before you leave town."

Michael watched as the two women with the fake Birkin bags stepped in front of Jets. She took their names and contact information. By the time she got to the assault victim she asked, "Bringing charges?"

"I don't think so," the woman replied. "Their humiliation at getting duped is enough for me. Sweet revenge thinking of them out four grand each just to carry around a fake alligator purse."

19

THE FINAL INTERVIEW

By the time Michael and Janis arrived at the constabulary, they found Robyn Fletcher sitting in a chair in the break room. She looked well put together in black jeans and a bright red cashmere turtleneck.

Michael felt awkward, knowing he'd be sitting in on the interview of his good friend's wife, a woman he'd known since he moved to Lily Rock, but also a woman who may have murdered a lady over a purse.

He wandered close to the refrigerator as Janis sat at the table across from Robyn. She placed her iPad on the table in front of her.

Michael fidgeted near the sink. *Do I just sit down and pretend to be Robyn's friend? How does this work anyway?* Jets spoke up first.

"I've asked Michael to sit in on the interviews. He's doing so in an official capacity, which means he won't talk to anyone else about what we say."

"Okay," mumbled Robyn.

Michael turned away from the counter, walking closer to sit down in the empty chair. He smiled at Robyn and then looked quickly at Jets. *I remember just last month having dinner with her and Thorny. We knocked back a few beers.* Then he remembered more. *Robyn left us by ourselves for a while, something on her computer, at least that's what she said. Thorny didn't mind.*

Michael had appreciated getting to know them both, especially Robyn. She had a solid presence. And he knew that she and Thorny made a good couple. Up until now he hadn't thought of them as anything but hardworking and dependable.

Jets leaned over to point toward the floor. "I notice you brought your purse," she said.

Robyn flushed. "I usually carry a bag, especially this time of year."

"Could I have a look?" Janis's question sounded more like a demand than an invitation.

Robyn reached down, bringing up a bag that looked much like the other women's, only hers was cobalt blue. "Here you go." She shoved it across the table at Jets, who immediately turned it over to look closely at the feet.

"They unscrew," she mumbled, turning one gold foot in her hand. She held it up for Michael to see.

"So what?" Robyn said.

"So this is another fake Birkin. Did you know it was a knockoff?" Jets screwed the foot back in.

"Since when do cops care about handbags?" Robyn shrugged. "I know it's a knockoff. I can't afford the real deal. But this one's good enough."

"Where did you get it?" Jets asked.

"Over the border. Thorny and I went to Mexico and he bought it for me. A street vendor, if you must know."

Jets's jaw tightened. "What I do know is that your bag," she pointed, "is the same basic design as the ones I've seen around town. Oh sure, they vary in color, but they are the same rectangular shape, made to look like they're constructed with crocodile, with gold feet and clasps. And I bet they're all knockoffs."

Robyn's demeanor changed. She pulled back into herself, her shoulders slumped around her small frame. "A lot of women love Birkins," she explained. But not in a convincing voice, more like an afterthought, as if even she knew she was making a lame excuse.

"That's true," Jets replied. "In fact I just spoke to two women this morning who told me all about Mrs. Claus. How she sold them Birkin bags at four thousand each, passing them off as the real deal. Of course four grand would be pricey for a purse, but if you think you're getting it at a huge bargain, it might be worth it, especially for Christmas."

Robyn's smile fell. No longer able to keep up the facade, her cheeks flushed and she turned her face away.

"Come on, Robyn, tell us," Jets urged. "How did you get into the purse business?"

When Robyn turned back around, her eyes were filled with tears. "We needed the money," she explained. "I lost a lot online. I gamble. Thorny doesn't know. I get time on the computer while he's busy with other things. Please don't tell him." She wiped at her eyes with her sleeve.

Michael inhaled deeply. *Jets has ferreted her way into her suspect's soft spot, the relationship with her husband. She's adept at going for the jugular. Remind me to stay on her good side.*

"But that's not all," Janis said evenly. "There's more that Thorny doesn't know, isn't there?" Jets lowered her voice, coaxing Robyn to agree. "Like how you killed Betty King. One shove of that nutcracker and she was done. Why did you do that anyway? Did Betty threaten to out your gambling and purse knockoff business to your husband?"

"Yes she did!" Robyn cried. "She knew about the purses and wanted a cut of my profit. That was okay, but then she asked for more and more money and when I finally said no, she told me she'd tell Thorny."

"So you unbolted the feet of the nutcracker. I bet you didn't intend to kill Betty, right? You just wanted to warn her..."

"I never expected her to die!" Robyn's eyes widened. "But I wasn't the only one who hated Betty King. She blackmailed all kinds of people, sending them notes to remind them of their payments. She'd even put their names on the ornaments of her tree.

"When they resisted giving her the payment, she'd nod to the tree and threaten them with something she knew. It was her sadistic way of making Christmas all about her profit. Once they'd paid in full, she handed over the ornament. She'd say, 'This is for you. I'll make another one for next year too. Be sure to stop by.'"

Does Robyn even realize she just admitted to murdering Betty King?

"I'm sure you didn't mean to kill her," Jets said, nodding, "but you kept trying nonetheless."

"I kept taking those screws out of the feet and they kept coming back. Then I realized it was Elf Two. He must have found the bolts the first time and then screwed them back into the deck. So I had to remove them again. The second time I learned my lesson and tossed the screws in the trash. I came back the next morning and damn, the nutcracker had been reinstalled just like before. What's the matter with that kid!"

"He needed to keep himself safe in that thing," Jets said

calmly. "You didn't think of that, how it would be unstable for him to stand in there when he was eavesdropping?"

Robyn's face contorted in anger. "It wasn't about him. My plan was to push the thing over on Betty first thing in the morning, before I had to pay her money to keep quiet. That's what she wanted, more than fifty percent of my operation's money.

"Since Betty had the same pattern every day, I knew when would be the best opportunity to take her out. Right before opening the shop, she'd step outside her door and stand there looking at the view."

"So that's when you finally got her. You must have gotten there earlier and hidden behind the nutcracker and then one solid push."

"And she was down." Robyn's eyes grew wide. "She must have died right there. When she didn't move I ran down the back stairs before anyone found her."

"Never thought to call an ambulance," Jets added. "Betty may still have been alive, but we'll never know." Looking over at Robyn, Jets began to type into her iPad.

Michael watched Robyn. Her eyes focused on her hands folded on the table. She only looked up when Janis stopped typing.

"I've got your statement. There's only one more question. Did you take the drill from Michael's truck and then give it to Logan to hide?"

Robyn looked over at Michael. "Sorry about that. I knew you had your tools in the truck bed, so I waited while you were busy in the market and took a chance. You didn't put the lock on securely, but then I'm not surprised. You're so distant this time of year. So I just took the drill. I would have put the stuff back, but Maguire showed up and I was afraid you'd be coming right along."

Michael felt his stomach clench. *She seems more concerned about the mess she made with my tools than the fact that she killed Betty King.*

Jets cleared her throat. "And just to make sure... You asked Logan to hide the drill?"

"Yes I did. Just so you know, I think he was relieved when Betty died."

Michael felt new admiration for Jets. *She knows how to pull the details out of a story bit by bit. Robyn has shown no sign of being defensive. In fact, she seems to be enjoying the confession, as if she doesn't realize the consequences.*

"One last thing," Jets added, "was Logan always part of your plan?"

"No, he wasn't part of my plan. He actually got in my way, putting the screws back every time I took them out."

Jets nodded. "Okay then. I'll make a note of that in my report." She closed out her document and stood. Without any warning, Jets reached over to take Robyn's arm. Her voice growled. "I am arresting you for the murder of Betty King. You have the right..."

Michael tuned out of the conversation. Robyn stood and Jets ushered her around through the doorway and down the hall toward the cells.

He heard a clank and then a door close. After that only silence remained.

20

CHRISTMAS MORNING

Michael came inside the house, Maguire at his heels. "Merry Christmas," Meadow greeted him. "Coffee and Christmas buns are in the kitchen. Come on in."

Maguire needed no further invitation. He trotted ahead of Michael to lead the way. Sage sat at the pine table, her hair curling over her shoulders, still in her pajamas. He looked at the pattern more closely.

"Reindeer and snowmen?" he asked.

Sage sighed. "It's Meadow. She gives me flannel PJs with a variety of Christmas motifs on Christmas Eve. I have a dozen just like these. And then every year in the spring I donate a set to the church jumble sale. She doesn't seem to mind."

"Mind what, dear?" Meadow asked, coming from the doorway. "Get Michael some coffee. I heard he's been working hard and has been quite helpful to Officer Jets."

Sage stood up. Pouring a mug of coffee, she placed it in front of Michael, who sat at the table. Before he could ask, she brought a pitcher of cream and the sugar bowl. "Here you go," she said, sitting back down.

The table had been set with a variety of cloth napkins, all

with a Christmas theme. Red and green, some purple—they'd been laundered and felt very soft to the touch. He slipped off a tree-shaped ring, placing the napkin on his lap.

"So it was Robyn who got arrested?" Sage took a sip of her coffee. Reaching to the center of the table, she lifted a platter full of cinnamon buns, decorated with red dots and green sprigs of holly, piped by Meadow early that morning. "Have a bun and then tell me everything."

Michael took one off the top. The buns smelled of cinnamon and vanilla. He placed it on a plate and then offered the plate to Sage, who smiled. By now Meadow joined them as Maguire bent over his bowl of breakfast kibble.

"News travels fast," Michael said. "I don't think I can tell you much more than you already know. Janis told me it was all confidential police business."

"But Robyn's in jail," answered Sage. "That news got out right away."

"We'll know more after the arraignment," he said before taking another bite of his bun.

Meadow looked thoughtful. "If you see Thorny, tell him I'll send over a plate of turkey with all the trimmings later today. They can have dinner together, even if it's in jail." She turned away from the table shaking her head.

Meadow's preoccupation with the dishes gave Sage a chance to lean closer to Michael. "You seem better this morning. Or are you just relieved that Christmas has finally arrived and that it's almost over?"

A day or two ago he might have brushed off her words by changing the subject. But this time he felt differently, as if he could share what was truly on his mind. "Things turned out better this year," he admitted. "I kept busy by helping people out. Maguire adopted me and made me feel loved. And you did too, you have a way of not intruding into my feelings but being unafraid of offering your support."

Sage smiled at him and leaned back in her chair. "So do you want to tell us what's going on with you? We're here you know, Meadow and me."

Meadow turned around from the sink, as if she'd been listening and knew her cue. Michael cleared his throat. "So before I moved to Lily Rock, I was married and..."

He felt his heart tighten. *Say his name. Just get it out there. These are your friends.* "And I had a son. His name was Daniel."

Now Meadow's eyes grew wide and then soft. Sage nodded, most likely anticipating what was coming next. "Daniel died five years ago. He had cancer. We tried everything but we couldn't save him. And then my wife, she needed space to grieve. I just bottled up my feelings and got back to work. Pretty soon we couldn't even see each other without fighting, because we only reminded each other of what we lost."

He rubbed his sleeve across his eyes. "So Christmas is the one time I can't ignore my feelings about Daniel. Plus just to make it even more difficult, his birthday is on December twenty-fifth. This is the one day when I remember who he was, how much I loved him. Daniel loved Christmas more than any other time of the year. That's why I'm moody and distant and not that much fun to be around."

Meadow spoke up first. "After what you've been through —losing a child and your marriage—I can't imagine what you've been feeling, especially at this time year. But so you know? Even moody Michael is good to have around."

Sage reached across the table, laying her hand on his. She nodded in agreement. "Plus you're so helpful when you're in a bad mood. Look at all the stuff you got done just this past week. Without you Janis may not have gotten Robyn to confess."

Aware of his heart's steady beat, he had to admit, *No one is talking me out of my feelings*. A surprising sense of peace came over him, then a welcome sense of letting go. "I appreciate how you don't think I'm unbearable." He grinned at Sage, then Meadow. "I also gotta say, I feel better telling you. Now I can think about Daniel and not keep him a secret. That's good." He looked down at his lap, then raised his eyes. "Very, very good," he repeated.

Reaching for another cinnamon roll, he asked, "Where's Avery and Logan? I thought they'd be up and scarfing down Christmas breakfast already."

"I called their parents," Meadow explained.

Sage chuckled. "Oh yeah, she did. Gave them a good talking to, like she would a kid with an overdue library book. Logan's mom came and picked them both up and took them back to Beverly Hills late last night."

"It was only appropriate," muttered Meadow. "Staying on location? Give me a break. What a sorry excuse for not being with loved ones."

Later that evening Michael stood in front of the fireplace at his cabin, staring into the bright flames. He looked at the mantel, filled with stones and pine cones that he'd picked up from his hikes. Walking across the room, he reached into the drawer of an old pine dresser. Photo frames skidded across the drawer. He picked out the red one right away.

With the elbow of his sleeve he polished the glass, staring at the photo of a boy sitting on Santa's lap, wearing a big grin, missing his two front teeth. He could hear Daniel call out, just as he had that day, "Hey, Dad. Santa says I'll get two new teeth for Christmas." The brightness of the voice had not faded in his memory, nor had his love for his son in that moment.

Michael took the photo, propping it on the mantel among the pine cones and rocks. Stepping back, he smiled at his son as his heart opened. He knew now that was not grief, that feeling in his chest. But the release of his love for Daniel flowing freely, something that he'd always feel.

There you go, kid. Back where you belong, in the center of my life where I can see you. In case you haven't figured it out, I'm living here now. I've found friends who are just like my family, but that doesn't mean I don't think of you every day. But I want you to know, I've stopped putting you away. Even if it hurts.

Welcome to Lily Rock, Daniel. I love you, son.

21

THE LILY ROCK TOWN COUNCIL

"Come to order," came Arlo's voice. "Welcome to the first Lily Rock town council meeting of the new year. The reading of the past minutes will be postponed for more urgent business. Michael Bellemare, you have the floor."

Michael stood behind his chair. "As you all know, over the holidays I came up with an idea that I think may work for our small town." He nodded to Maguire, who sat in the middle of a stage, a big smile on his lips, his tongue hanging out the side of his mouth.

"Go on, dear," Meadow urged.

"Yeah, get to the point," grumbled Doc.

"Maguire has gotten to the age that he no longer wants to stay at home. Like any good boy, he likes getting around town, greeting residents, stopping for the odd meal, begging treats off of strangers. In order to accommodate his special gifts of friendliness and to keep him safe, I suggest that he's the perfect choice to be a spokes-dog for our community."

All eyes looked over at the dog, who stood up on his back legs, poised to be the center of attention.

"He likes to be the most important," Skye mumbled.

Michael cleared his throat. "I did some research and discovered that Lily Rock is too small to have a mayor."

"We tried to get Doc to be our mayor, but Riverside told us no," said Skye.

Michael waited to see if any of them knew where he was going. When no one else interrupted, he continued. "And I'm also aware that Maguire here is costing Meadow a pretty penny because she has to bail him out of animal rescue whenever he's spotted off lead."

"It's against the county regulations," remarked Skye, "to let a dog go off lead."

"It's my suggestion that we take up a vote today to appoint our first political representative—not your everyday choice, but one that suits us quite nicely."

"Could I still be his handler?" Meadow asked. She now seemed to realize where Michael was headed.

"He'll need a deputy," Michael agreed.

"And he can stay with me?" Meadow wondered aloud.

"Or wherever he wants to stay. When he's at my house I'll text you so you won't worry," Michael added.

"Oh yeah, we can do that," Arlo agreed. "Text you if he picks one of us. No problem."

"So what do you say. Do we have a consensus? Is everyone on board?"

All heads nodded an affirmation.

"That's good." Michael dug in his pocket, pulling out a bandanna. "Who wants to tell Maguire about his new job description and tie this around his neck?"

"I will." Meadow stood up. She walked closer to the dog, who offered her his paw. "Treat later," she warned him. Reaching around his neck, she tied the red bandanna so that the words appeared on his furry chest. Meadow turned around, revealing a wide smile.

"Everyone, I'd like you to meet the most agreeable political appointment to ever grace a town. Say hello to Mayor Maguire."

"Meeting adjourned," commanded Arlo. "Dog treats all around."

* * *

Thank you for reading *All Aboard for Murder*! For the latest Lily Rock news join my VIP newsletter. PS signing up also gets you a copy of *Meadow's Hat*, a short story set before book one :).

Sign up on bonniehardywrites.com/newsletter

Start the Lily Rock Mystery series with *Getaway Death*

Prologue

Overheard in Lily Rock

"I love the town of Lily Rock. Their lies are so authentic."

Fog rolled over the mountain road. Despite the poor visibility, the woman drove as if her life depended upon it.

A sharp curve to the right—her squealing tires issued a warning.

Tentatively removing one hand from the steering wheel, she kept her eyes on the road, her fingers reaching down for her windshield wipers. *Swish.* The blade on the glass moved to the left, then the right. Her gaze remained fixed on the road in front of her. Reaching over the steering wheel, she swiped with her hand at the thick condensation blocking her view from inside the car.

Veering into the next curve, she felt her stomach lurch. Brakes squealed again as the car catapulted into an unexpected second hairpin turn. Her head lolled to the right. As she came out of the curve, she pushed the button on the foggy driver's side door and rolled down the window, revealing clouds of fog.

Another vehicle rumbled behind her car, close to her bumper.

"I guess somebody's in a big hurry," she snapped to the empty car.

The window slid shut as she looked out of the front windshield to the right, then the left. No turnout lane yet. Tightness stiffened her neck as her hands began to shake on the wheel. *Stop tailgating me. Please.*

She felt the tires slip on the road, the car floating for a moment. As she slammed on the brakes, her body heaved against the seat belt, her neck and head rocking forward then back. Her stomach came up to her throat.

As her car skidded toward the cliff, she only had one thought:

I finally know how I will die.

End of Sample

To continue reading, be sure to pick up *Getaway Death* at your favorite retailer.

Along with contests, discounts, giveaways, and events, I'll send you *Meadow's Hat,* a free short story download.

Signup on bonniehardywrites.com/newsletter.

Lily Rock Mystery Series

Olivia Greer's trip to the mountain town of Lily Rock turns out quite differently than the getaway she expected. Her friend is found dead and she ends up being the prime suspect in the murder. With the help of Mayor Maguire, the town's labradoodle, and Michael Bellemare, the famous hunky architect, she comes to discover deep connections to the town that she could never have anticipated. Love. Laughter. Whodunit. Join Olivia as she begins her journey of self discovery.

Welcome to Lily Rock Holiday Mystery Series

Holiday Cozy Mystery Novellas

As an homage to the holiday classic film, *It's a Wonderful Life,* Bonnie Hardy contemplates what the small town of Lily Rock was like before the arrival of Olivia Greer. In this prequel spin-off series, you'll enjoy fresh adventures with holiday themes and learn the backstories of the characters you've come to know and love.

Redondo and Rose Neighbors in Crime

He's a mentalist. She's a doula. They are neighbor's in crime.

In this new series by Bonnie Hardy, Neighbors Rex Redondo and Vivienne Rose are entangled in the investigation of who murdered the woman floating in Viv's swimming pool. Playing Bogart to her Bacall, Rex and Viv solve the mystery and explore their mid-life romance in a setting reminiscent of Old Hollywood.

ACKNOWLEDGMENTS

Like Michael Bellemare, not everyone enjoys the holiday season. Many people feel a sense of disconnect and a missing at this time of year.

My hope is that *All Aboard for Murder* will not only satisfy the joy in solving a good mystery, but that it will also gently remind you that you are not alone during this holiday season.

Many people miss loved ones at Christmas, people who no longer grace our dinner table. Like some of you, I've struggled to keep upbeat just like Michael. And like Michael, I've become more resilient over the years. But traveling from loss and despair, to hope and acceptance isn't easy.

It's only been recently that I no longer feel the need to push aside my sadness. I've learned to welcome nearly all of my feelings including longing, happiness and joy, along with melancholy and missing, sometimes in the same day.

Surrounded by friends and family I've come to accept myself more fully no matter what my mood. And that's why I think Meadow says it best when she's speaking to Michael at the end of this book:

"I can't imagine what you've been feeling, especially at this time year. But so you know? Even moody Michael is good to have around."

Thanks to Kate Tilton, Christie Stratos, and Husband for all of their assistance and help.

May all of you who love the characters in Lily Rock have a joy filled holiday. And may you return to this book when you need a boost in spirit, realizing that you, like sometimes-crabby Michael, are not alone.

Happy Reading,
Bonnie

ABOUT THE AUTHOR

Born and raised in Los Angeles, Bonnie Hardy is a educator, curriculum writers, musician, , and preacher. A lover of libraries and literacy, Bonnie directed a literacy center in her home town.

Bonnie has published in *Christian Century*, *Presence: An International Journal for Spiritual Direction*, and with Pilgrim Press. She's written numerous short stories some which can be found on her Facebook page.

When not planting flowers and baking cookies, she's sitting at her computer plotting her next cozy mystery.

You can connect with Bonnie at
bonniehardywrites.com

www.ingramcontent.com/pod-product-compliance
Lightning Source LLC
Chambersburg PA
CBHW030838200726
48285CB00007B/2475